THE COST OF SENSIBILITY

By Joy Michelle Austin

DEDICATION

Dedicated to my dearest friends who have been my truest champions and supporters. This is a story of friendship and I hope they know just how much I value each of our friendships.

COPYRIGHT

The Cost of Sensibility

© 2026 by Joy Michelle Austin

All rights reserved.

This novel is a work of fiction. Any resemblance to actual persons, living or deceased, is purely coincidental, except where historical or public figures are referenced. The characters, events, and locations are either products of the author's imagination or used fictitiously for the purpose of storytelling.

This book was inspired by the characters of Jane Austen and reimagined in a modern setting, as well as the true story of Elisabeth Fritzl, whose strength and survival in the face of unimaginable darkness deeply influenced the themes of endurance, faith, and redemption in this novel.

For permissions, inquiries, or to connect with the author, e-mail:

thejoyousauthor@thejoyousliving.com

First Edition: January 2026

Printed in the United States of America

Table of Contents

WORD OF WARNING

This story includes themes of **trauma, abuse, pregnancy loss, and grief.** Please read with care and at your own pace.

If you or someone you know has experienced abuse or sexual violence, confidential help is available.

United States:
Call or text **988** to reach the Suicide & Crisis Lifeline (24/7)
Call **1-800-656-HOPE (4673)** or visit RAINN.org to reach the National Sexual Assault Hotline

United Kingdom & Ireland:
Call Samaritans at **116 123** or visit samaritans.org

Australia:
Call Lifeline at **13 11 14** or visit lifeline.org.au

Elsewhere:
Visit https://www.opencounseling.com/suicide-hotlines to find local crisis resources by country.

If this story has touched something tender for you, please know that support is available. Speaking with a trusted counselor, pastor, or trained advocate can be an important step toward healing. If you or someone you know needs immediate help, the resources listed above can connect you with confidential support.

You are not alone.

Help is available, and healing is possible.

PROLOGUE

Rick couldn't stop smiling as he took in the greatest moment of his life.

Strains of Prokofiev drifted through the backyard, the orchestral notes lifting and falling beneath lanterns strung overhead. Laughter carried from somewhere behind him. Best of all was the quiet, grounding weight of Marianne's wedding band, pressed warm against his skin.

Then the sound shifted. It did not happen all at once, only enough for his body to notice before his mind caught up.

Just outside the circle of the impromptu dance floor, Lucy Ferrars stood too quickly and swayed instantaneously. Anxiety shot through Rick as he turned to the scene at once.

She had gone pale, her smile pulled thin as she pressed one hand low against her abdomen. Her husband Eddie hovered beside her, frozen, his face already drained of color.

"Lucy?" someone called as the music wavered and a chair scraped back.

Pastor Fanny was suddenly there, her voice calm and clear enough to cut through the rising confusion. "No! Whatever you do, don't move."

Before Rick could take another step forward, his own bride was already moving. Marianne crossed the yard with purpose, her focus locked on her friend. Uncaring of her wedding dress, she knelt in front of Lucy and lifted one steady, reassuring hand.

"Hey," Marianne said gently. "I'm right here. Take deep breaths for me, please."

Lucy's breath came shallow. "I—I feel dizzy."

Marianne's eyes moved quickly as if she was cataloging Lucy's color and posture, as well as the protective curve of Lucy's arm over her abdomen. "Okay. That's all right. Stay with me. Slow breaths, darling."

Rick stood just behind her, close enough to hear the even cadence of Marianne's voice, near enough to see Eddie's hands shaking at Lucy's side.

"Eddie," Marianne said without looking up, composed but firm. "I need you to listen."

He nodded too fast. "Yes."

"I need you to go to the driveway and help direct the paramedics back here when they arrive. Can you do that for Lucy?"

He nodded and rushed out with a friend. With a grimace, Marianne turned her attention back to Lucy.

"Are you having pain? Cramping? Any bleeding?"

Lucy swallowed. "Pain. It's low and – oh gosh, Marianne! I'm so scared. What's going to happen to my baby?"

Marianne nodded once. "Okay. We're not panicking. But we are going to the hospital."

Phones came out, and whispers rippled. Someone said Marianne's name again, unnecessarily.

"I'll drive," Rick offered.

"No," Pastor Fanny said at once.

All eyes turned to her.

She stepped forward, placing a steady hand over Rick's own hand. Her voice stayed level, pastoral and unyielding. "I will drive. We don't want the bride and groom coming to the hospital as you have a flight to catch in several hours."

Rick looked at her, stunned. "I'd completely forgotten."

"Well, thankfully, I hadn't forgotten," Fanny reassured him. "Ned already called emergency when it all started so they should be here—oh perfect. I think I hear the sirens now."

Marianne glanced up and gave a single approving nod. "Thank you, Fanny. I'm just going to go talk to them for a minute. Rick, why don't you sit here with Lucy until they load her up?"

Rick hovered close as Lucy groaned and moaned as more pain pulsed through her body.

He squeezed Lucy's shoulder. "You're not alone," he said quietly. "Look at all these people praying for you and your family. You guys are loved."

Tears slipped free as she nodded. "I'm sorry. We ruined your beautiful wedding."

"You didn't ruin anything," Rick said. "Just go take care of yourself and we'll see you in Bath in a couple weeks. Okay?"

Within a couple minutes, Rick watched as if in slow motion as the ambulance door closed. Gravel crunched beneath the tires. Then the taillights disappeared down the drive.

Rick stayed where he was for a moment longer, the echo of the engine hanging in the quiet.

Behind him, the wedding lights still glowed. His children had gathered close, solemn and silent. Marianne returned to his side, slipping her hand into his, her thumb brushing once against his palm—a quiet check-in.

Nearby, Pastor Ned's voice rose, calling family and friends to prayer. Rick bowed his head, his breathing still uneven. He did not know what waited at the hospital, but he knew this truth with certainty: Eddie would not face it alone.

PART I

Rick's Journal

Some days the bravest thing a man can do is walk into a room he doesn't feel worthy of. I've learned that showing up—tired, hurting, unfinished—isn't weakness. It's how healing starts.

CHAPTER ONE

I used to think healing was a finish line, some ceremony where everything broken snapped back into place overnight. I am learning that it does not work that way.

Most days, healing looks smaller and quieter. It shows up in pancakes at sunrise, footsteps overhead, and Ellie laughter in my ear tickling me awake before the fear has time to settle in.

Rescue was God's miracle. Learning how to live after it feels like kindness still unfolding. I did not know yet how much more that mercy would be tested.

Something small tapped Rick's shoulder, and his body reacted before his mind caught up.

White-hot lightning split his chest as the old terrors surged, bringing with them the memory of a cold floor, metal constricting around his neck, and the feeling of disgrace tightening as Louisa made free use of his body whether he wanted her to or not.

"Daddy! Wake uuup!"

His eyes snapped open.

He was not surrounded by concrete walls nor darkness. It was his Ellie sitting up on his bed. They were safe in Darcy's beach cottage. *How could he have forgotten?*

Her round face hovered inches from his, hair sticking up like a startled duckling. Quackers lay sprawled across his pillow, the duck wedged between them as if standing guard, loyal and unmoving.

Rick forced a slow breath through his nose. Then another. His pulse still raced, but the panic loosened its grip faster than it once had. He pushed onto one elbow as Ellie climbed into his arms, warm and solid, her weight grounding him before his thoughts fully caught up.

Her hands cupped his face as she sweetly pressed butterfly kisses against his cheeks. One after another her kisses brought him back to reality.

"Morning, Little Love," he said, his voice still rough with his nightmare.

She giggled, soft and unafraid. "Can we have pancakes?"

"That depends," Rick said. "Is Quackers still mad I ate the last bite yesterday?"

Ellie gasped. "He forgave you. He loves you, Daddy."

Rick smiled, the kind that came slowly but refused to leave once it arrived. "That's a relief."

Footsteps thundered overhead causing Ellie to giggle as she pointed above their heads. "Elephants!"

Rick couldn't help but laugh as he swung her into his arms for a hug. The house vibrated with life, with motion, with belonging. His sons were awake and already in motion, followed by their elder sister. Lily's squeal cut through the ceiling, sharp enough to rattle the windows.

It was hard to believe that just a month ago they had moved into his best friend's beach cottage in Croft Beach, trading borrowed rooms and temporary spaces for a place that finally felt like theirs, for the insane price of one dollar a month. Sunlight streamed through wide windows. Salt air drifted in from the beach, fresh and clean.

Had it really already been ten months since he had first tasted freedom?

Rick lay there longer than necessary, staring at the ceiling fan as it turned lazily above him. Morning light crept in around the edges of the curtains heralding a new year. The house always felt different in the daylight. The sight of the sun and clouds would never get old after ten years of captivity in Louisa's basement.

He pressed his palm flat to his chest, grounding himself in the steady thud beneath it. He was alive. He was here in his own home. He and the children were safe.

The counselor had taught him to name what was real before his thoughts could spiral backward.

Ellie's warmth.

The weight of the blankets.

The distant crash of waves outside the windows.

Rick breathed through each truth slowly, deliberately, until the knot between his shoulders loosened.

Healing, he was discovering, did not move in a straight line. Some mornings he woke ready to take on the day. Others, the night clung to him like a second skin, and it took effort just to sit up. He used to measure progress by how little he thought about the cellar. Now he measured it by how quickly he was able to return to the present.

Today, he was winning. The thought surprised him enough that he smiled faintly. Maybe this was what mercy looked like when it stayed.

Ellie curled against his chest as she traced circles on his sleep shirt with the solemn focus of someone doing important work. "I dreamed about Miss Marianne," she whispered. "She had a sparkly dress, and we were dancing."

"She'll love hearing that," Rick said. "Think you would be okay dancing with your old man at the wedding, Little Love?"

She giggled and nodded exuberantly before kissing his whiskered chin.

Once he had shaved and brushed his teeth, Rick carried Ellie into the living room, where chaos had already taken root. At the center of the room, Walter stood lecturing Sam with the seriousness of a drill sergeant twice his size.

"If you put syrup on before the waffles are toasted, they taste like soggy socks."

"I like soggy socks," Sam argued.

"No you don't—" Walter argued as Ellie piped up simultaneously that she wanted pancakes and not waffles.

"HEY!" Sam jabbed a finger. "Dad, Walter said I don't like soggy socks!"

Rick tried and failed to hold back a smile as he sat Ellie down and raised both hands in surrender. "No one in this house likes soggy socks. Especially if it's something we have to eat. I especially don't like soggy socks before I've had a decent cup of coffee."

Lily, nine years old and bright-eyed, burst into the kitchen fast on his heels with Maggie Dashwood trailing behind her. Marianne's younger sister wore unicorn pajamas, and her raven-haired pigtails bounced when she moved.

"Bonjour, soon-to-be-brother-in-law!"

Rick blinked as he turned away from the coffee maker. "Why French?"

"Because I'm cool."

Lily groaned. "We watched *Ratatouille* last night, and now she thinks she's French."

Rick laughed, the sound easy and unguarded, and turned back to the coffee maker. "Think you can whip up some breakfast, Chef Maggie?"

"Um, I don't know how to say yes in French." Maggie frowned.

"It's *oui*," Rick pronounced as he handed the girls the waffle mix and grabbed a carton of eggs from the fridge. "Let me know if you girls need me to reach anything."

"Oui, oui," Lily and Maggie chorused in a fit of giggles as Rick and Ellie wandered back into the living room to check on the boys.

Soon, the scent of cinnamon and nutmeg filled the air. Rick peeked into the kitchen where the girls were busy practicing their flipping skills to the detriment of the eggs. He chuckled as he grabbed an orange from the counter and headed back to keep an eye on the other three.

A year ago, Lily didn't even know what a spatula was and cried herself to sleep because she wanted her chain removed. Now the house rang with laughter, with spilled batter and teasing words, and the weight of that contrast pressed in hard enough to steal his breath for a moment.

He did not deserve this.

As if she felt the swell of the moment too, Lily wrapped her arms around his middle without warning and squeezed tight. Rick rested his hand on her head and breathed through the ache until it softened.

"Happy New Year, Sweetheart," he said, pressing a kiss to her forehead.

"Happy New Year, Daddy."

A knock sounded at the door.

Rick had not realized how much he had been listening for that sound until it came.

"That's Marianne's knock!" Maggie shouted from the counter, where she was pouring batter into the waffle maker.

Rick felt like a schoolboy excited to see his date for the eighth-grade dance as he swung the door open to reveal the woman who had made his dreams come true. Marianne stood on the porch in a soft pink sweater dress with knee high leather boots and a denim jacket capping the ensemble. She had never looked more beautiful, he thought. Her cheeks were flushed from the cold, carrying a to-go carrier filled with coffee cups and a pink box from Mrs. Jennings' bakery.

When she stepped inside, her gaze swept the room, taking in the chaos and cheer before landing on the sight of her younger sister and Lily arguing over how many more waffles they needed to make.

"You brought bribery," Rick said with a grin, pointing to the box in her hand.

"I brought coffee," she corrected. "And orange scones."

Ellie barreled into her legs from the living room, and with a chuckle Marianne handed off the coffee and scones before reaching down to scoop her up. Watching Marianne love his children with that same steady, unforced warmth she'd shown when rescuing them from the cellar made Rick's heart pound with pride and joy. The contrast between Marianne's safety and sweetness and Louisa's cruelty and coldness was stark as night and day.

Setting Ellie down, Marianne moved easily through the room and into the kitchen, where she naturally took over helping the girls finish breakfast. She poured juice while tutoring them on the best technique for flipping an egg, patient and encouraging.

"Where's Elinor?" Maggie asked once they had all sat down to eat.

Marianne's fork paused halfway to her mouth. "She had something come up. She said she'd see us later."

The words landed easily enough, but Rick noticed the way her smile seemed to set rather than soften, as though she had already decided how the moment needed to look.

"I suppose we're all running late today," Lily said, glancing toward the empty chairs. "Pastor Eddie and Lucy aren't here yet either."

Marianne nodded, reaching for her water glass. "Lucy texted me earlier saying they might not make it. She wasn't feeling well again."

Rick nodded as he thought about the similar text he'd received from Eddie.

Walter leaned forward, blissfully unaware of timing or tension. "Is Mrs. Lucy going to have her baby before your wedding?"

Rick froze and coughed on the waffle he had just bitten into.

"They haven't told everyone yet," he explained carefully. "It's their news, so for now we pray for Pastor Eddie and Lucy and the baby, and keep it to ourselves. Okay?"

Five solemn heads nodded in agreement, and the conversation naturally turned to questions about the engagement.

"When are you getting married?"

"Will Miss Marianne be our mom?"

"Where will we live?"

"One question at a time," Rick laughed as Marianne nudged his knee beneath the table.

"I might already have a date in mind," he added, a twinkle in his eye.

Ignoring that news, Maggie pointed her fork at him. "Are you my brother now?"

"I guess I will be when your sister does me the honor of marrying me."

"I can live with that."

Laughter filled the room, questions overlapping, answers half-finished, when another knock sounded.

Moments later, Caroline swept in wearing emerald green, Darcy behind her with a box of donuts and a gift bag.

"So," Darcy said, clapping Rick's shoulder. "Engaged life treating you well?"

Before Rick could answer, Fanny Bertram peeked around the corner and was soon joined by Pastor Ned, who carried a casserole dish.

"We thought we'd start the year together," Fanny explained. "Looks like everyone had the same idea."

Rick shook Ned's hand and hurried to grab extra chairs. "What's the occasion?"

"Two occasions, actually," Fanny said. "First, celebrations are in order after yesterday's wedding and proposal. Second, we'd love to invite all the adults to a marriage retreat this spring in Bath, England."

Rick's chest tightened. England meant distance. It suggested new rooms. There'd be fresh locks for him to figure out how to open. Too many unknowns crowded in his mind.

He crouched beside Ellie, gathering crumbs that did not need his immediate attention, slowing his breathing until the room steadied.

"No pressure to say yes right this moment," Fanny said gently, patting his shoulder. "I think the more thrilling question is—when is your wedding?"

"February twenty-eighth."

The room went still.

Marianne turned to him, eyes bright and wide.

Rick cleared his throat. "I was kind of hoping I could talk her into marrying me next month."

"Of course I'll marry you on the twenty-eighth," Marianne sobbed, throwing her arms around his neck.

Rick pressed his forehead to hers, breathing her in until the room came back into focus.

Later, after the house emptied and the older kids were busy playing in the den, Rick tucked a sleepy Ellie into bed with her stuffed animals. He could not resist curling up beside her, listening to her soft breaths and watching her chest rise and fall.

Between chasing the kids, counseling sessions, work at Darcy's firm, physical therapy, and the emotional weight healing demanded, Rick fell into bed most nights like he had run a marathon in sand.

The times he could nap beside Ellie felt heaven-sent. He loved most of all the sight of his baby sleeping in a real bed, wrapped in warm blankets and surrounded by stuffed animals.

Unfortunately, his thoughts drifted. They turned to his good friend and mentor-cum-pastor, Eddie Ferrars. Something had been off the other night, and even though their reasons for not being able to join the Wentworths for breakfast made sense, something still tickled at his brain.

Rick hated the instinctive tightening in his gut when he thought about it. He had spent months learning to trust his senses again, to distinguish between fear born of memory and concern rooted in reality. This felt like the latter, however. It was like the moment just before a storm when the air pressed heavier against the skin.

He replayed fragments of the evening in his mind. Eddie's smile that hadn't quite reached his eyes. Lucy's hand resting protectively on her barely visible belly. Elinor's laughter, too quick, followed by a silence that lingered longer than it should have. He had nothing concrete he could point to and name without sounding paranoid.

And yet.

Rick had lived too long in a place where small changes meant everything. A door left ajar. A footstep out of rhythm. The way a voice shifted when a lie was forming. Survival had trained him to notice what others missed, and while he hated that part of himself, he could not dismiss it either.

Rick did not want trouble and as he glanced toward Ellie's sleeping face he felt the familiar surge of resolve. Whatever storms lay ahead, he would not let them undo the life they were building. Not for himself and certainly not for his children. And not for the people he loved, even when loving them meant asking hard questions.

Especially then.

"Daddy?"

Rick looked up.

Lily, Walter, and Sam stood lined up in front of him, hands tucked behind their backs like a jury about to deliver a verdict. Beside him, Ellie lifted her sleepy head and tucked her thumb into her mouth, studying her siblings.

The memory of last night flickered—construction paper signs, Darcy's smirk, Marianne's stunned laugh when the kids announced he already had the ring.

"I'm not sure I can handle any more surprises," Rick said cautiously, sitting up, "after the one you pulled last night."

Walter frowned. "But you wanted to ask her, right?"

"Of course I did. I just had something different in mind. Yours was better though. Hands down."

Sam rocked on his heels. "Well… aren't you curious what we have for you now?"

Rick arched a brow. "I'm terrified. But sure."

"You have to guess!" Ellie squealed, crawling into his lap.

"Is it a doghouse for Daniel?"

"No!" Lily huffed as the puppy barreled into the room. "Daniel doesn't belong in a doghouse."

"New fishing pole?"

Walter rolled his eyes. "If anyone gets one, it's me."

Rick lifted his hands. "I surrender."

"Ta-da!" they shouted.

Lily pulled the festive gift bag Darcy had brought earlier from behind her back.

"Uncle Darcy gave it to us!" Sam said proudly.

Rick smiled as he parted the tissue paper. Something sharp brushed his fingers. Looking down in surprise, he pulled out a picture frame and turned it over.

His breath caught. His eyes burned.

Some moments did not heal a man. They broke him open in the best ways possible, and mercy slipped in through the cracks.

CHAPTER TWO

Text Message from Rick to Eddie

You are missed.

Eddie stared at his phone for a long moment before turning it face down on the kitchen table. It should not have hurt, especially because Rick always meant well. He always chose his words carefully and sent them without expectation, and never demanded a reply. A man like that should have been easy to answer. Instead, Eddie sat alone at the breakfast table and whispered into the empty room, "I don't know if I'll ever be ready to face it."

Lucy had already gone out despite the late night they had at the wedding. At dawn, the bedroom door had opened just wide enough for her to step into the hall. She wore one of her beautiful flowing dresses that they'd found at the maternity shop, hair twisted into a loose knot. Her face looked softer than it had in weeks, and he had an urge to sweet-talk her back into bed for the rest of the day but her eyes never lifted to meet his.

"I'm going to do some shopping," she had muttered.

He wanted to remind her that the shops wouldn't be open at this early hour, but she had put up a wall and he was unsure how he could break it down.

"Do you want breakfast?" he remembered asking in a last-ditch attempt. "We could go grab something before your shopping?"

"I'm not hungry."

The door closed before he could come up with any other excuse to keep her with him.

Three hours had passed with no sign of Lucy, and the house was way too still. There was no hint of Lucy's playlist humming through the speakers as it was sure to do at most waking hours. The scent of her sweet strawberry lotion wasn't lingering in the hallway or kitchen either. Only the faint chime of the church bells next door drifted through the kitchen window he'd cracked open.

They both knew why she was avoiding him and yet Eddie refused to believe it could be as bad as all that.

He had not gone looking to betray Lucy. He told himself that he had not even been the one to initiate the kiss last night. Was it really his fault if an ex-girlfriend kissed him after having had a few too many drinks?

Shaking his head as he grabbed his keys and hoodie from the hook, Eddie sighed as the simple truth pressed on his ribs.

Elinor still hoped, and the knowledge tightened his jaw.

And, darn it, but he had done nothing to kill that hope since she'd arrived in town last month. Scratch that, Eddie growled as he locked the front door behind him. He'd done everything to kill that hope by marrying another woman. Wasn't that enough of a reason to let hope die? What more did Elinor want from him?

Kicking at a pebble as he crossed to the church, Eddie felt like kicking himself.

He was fooling himself if he thought he was blameless in all of this. It was his very own silence on the subject since Elinor's untimely arrival in town that had given her room to dream again, and that silence had driven a spear into Lucy's heart. He sure didn't earn husband of the year by letting his pregnant wife carry the weight of his silence through nausea, fatigue, and the quiet terror of early pregnancy.

If only Marianne and Caroline had not seen it. He had frozen at the sight of Marianne and Caroline's twin looks of shock and disappointment as Lucy's voice drifted towards him at the same time, calling his name as she returned to retrieve the sweater she'd forgotten.

He groaned and dragged a hand through his hair as he sat down heavily in his office chair. Even his office felt cold and barren. With the staff given the day off for the holiday, there would be no work done today. Sighing, he stood and headed into the empty sanctuary and slipped into the back pew, head bowed.

"I figured you might be here."

Pastor Ned Bertram nodded his head in greeting before sitting down next to Eddie in the pew.

Eddie straightened. "I wasn't hiding."

Ned let the words hang there as he glanced toward the front of the sanctuary. "I've known you long enough to know that you always come here, Ferrars, when you don't know what to do next."

Eddie's face burned. He kept his eyes on the worn wood of the pew, his hands folded too tightly in his lap. After a quiet moment, Eddie spoke up. "Did Fanny tell you that several people witnessed Elinor Dashwood kissing me last night?"

Ned didn't react with surprise. He only exhaled and looked up at the cross at the front of the sanctuary. "No, but you just did."

"I can't preach Sunday," Eddie groaned. "I can't stand up there pretending I am worthy of being God's mouthpiece." His voice caught. "I need time away from the pulpit. Time to make amends to Lucy… and Elinor. I need to turn my feet the right direction before I tell anyone else how to walk."

Ned's expression deepened into something steady and solemn as he listened to Eddie ramble on. "And what direction are your feet turning?"

Eddie closed his eyes briefly, then opened them with effort. "I don't know. All I know is that I need someone I trust to step in for me. It'll just be for a little while. It feels like a God thing that you and Fanny are in town." His voice broke. "I wouldn't normally ask but I need your help."

Ned studied him. "You're asking me to preach?"

"Yes," Eddie said. "If—if you're willing."

Ned nodded, slow and sure. "I am. But what about Collins?"

"He'd be happy to preach, I'm sure, but I'd rather not have to talk to him about it."

Ned leaned back against the pew. "Time away will give you space. Avoiding the reason why won't, however, fix whatever this is."

"I just need to rest. It's not that big of a deal. I'll tell the elders and staff that I'm taking a sabbatical to rest for a few weeks."

"You're not asking for rest," Ned said. "You're asking for time to sort this mess out. But what's the point?"

"Point?"

"Yes." Ned nodded. "Why do you need time if you know what's got to be fixed?"

Eddie swallowed. "If I tell the truth about my feelings, I might lose her."

"If you don't tell the truth," Ned replied softly, "you already risk that."

They sat in stillness before Ned spoke again.

"Miss Dashwood may be someone from your past that you loved at one time. But she is not your wife. Lucy is."

Eddie swallowed and nodded once more. Just as Eddie was opening his mouth to refute the notion that he had forgotten which of these women was his wife, Ned pushed himself upright.

"Go home. Tell Lucy everything. If you need help turning your feet, I'll gladly walk with you." He squeezed Eddie's shoulder gently and smiled.

Eddie's shoulders sagged, then slowly straightened as he looked up at Ned with the briefest of smiles.

"Sermon concluded," Ned said, clapping Eddie on the shoulder. "See you on Sunday."

Eddie walked back home in silence. Lucy's car was still gone. The house remained still. He sat for a long time with his forehead pressed against the bedroom wall, trying to sort his thoughts. Then, slowly, he reached for his phone.

He stared at the message for a long moment after sending it, the familiar instinct to soften the truth rising in his chest. He pushed it down.

Choosing Lucy would mean laying everything bare—his fear, his silence, and the feelings he had been too afraid to name aloud. It would mean closing a door he had foolishly left cracked open and accepting whatever consequences waited on the other side. Eddie bowed his head, pressing his forehead against the wall as he whispered a prayer not for escape, but for courage. If healing was going to begin, it would have to start with truth.

He only hoped he had the strength to live up to his own expectations.

Chapter Three

"Walk, Ellie. You have to walk. Pastor Fanny said no running near the ducks."

"This *is* walking," Ellie said, breathless. "Fast walking."

Lily snorted. "That's sprinting, Duckling."

From the park bench, Rick watched Lily and Maggie supervising Ellie as she tried to follow the ducks around the pond while Walter and Sam kick a soccer ball back and forth. Thank goodness for Ned and Fanny Bertram who had offered to supervise with the ease of seasoned saints. Ned nodded toward Rick as if to say *go on, enjoy the morning,* and Rick let himself breathe.

That's when he saw her. Marianne walked up the path toward him with sunlight in her raven tresses, carrying a wedding binder tucked against her side. She was casually attired in a pair of skinny denim jeans and a soft cream-colored sweater that accentuated her natural beauty. She was one of the only women Rick knew who could look perfect even without a face full of makeup.

She smiled when she reached him, and something inside Rick tilted toward her, the way a compass rights itself.

"Hi," she grinned.

"Hi." He nodded at the binder. "Should I be scared?"

"Probably." Her grin turned wickedly sweet. "I made a spreadsheet."

He feigned horror. "And I thought I was marrying into calm domesticity."

"You chose chaos," she teased. "Beautiful, organized chaos."

They sat close, hips brushing. Her presence grounded him in a way he still couldn't fully put into words.

Across the pond, Ellie marched dramatically with Ned while Lily and Maggie tossed frozen peas in graceful arcs at the ducks. The scene felt complete, in a way he didn't question.

And then the memory of yesterday's surprise flickered through him—sharp and tender.

The breath had left Rick's lungs when he'd seen the photo the children gave him. It had been a picture of his parents, young and laughing in the California sun on their own wedding day nearly forty years earlier. His mother's veil had blown sideways by the wind. His father's hand appeared steady at her waist.

But what Rick couldn't unsee was the look of absolute love between his parents as they fondly looked into each other's eyes. He could only hope that his children would see that same kind of love when they saw wedding photos of Marianne and himself.

It amazed him to think that Darcy had somehow conjured up that photo. Rick hadn't seen the picture since just before Louisa kidnapped him almost eleven years ago. When his mom had died, while Rick had been locked away in Louisa's cellar, everything of hers had been packed away in a rush of grief.

Thank God for best friends like Darcy who had gathered everything up into boxes and tucked them into his own attic. He had kept every receipt, photo, and treasure from Rick's mom's apartment with the belief that Rick would one day make his way home to Croft Beach.

When the world had given up on him, Darcy hadn't.

"Hey," Marianne murmured, nudging his knee. "Where'd you go?"

He shook his head. "Thinking about the gift the kids gave me yesterday."

Her expression softened. "The picture? I can't wait to see it."

"Yeah." His voice dropped. "It meant more than I can say."

She slipped her hand into his, squeezing his own.

"I had hoped we could sort things out for the wedding but you know what?"

"What?"

"I think we'd be better off spending today with the kids. Should we round everyone up for a game of soccer?"

He huffed softly. "Sounds amazing but if we are getting married on February Twenty-Eighth, we don't have much time."

"We have all the supplies from Darcy and Caroline's wedding and we could even keep all the lights up until then."

"I don't know what I did to deserve an angel like you," he sighed as he leaned in to press his lips against her soft ones. "Marianne, I know I looked uncertain about the retreat. I won't deny that the idea did scare me at the beginning. Unfortunately, even good things can trigger panic. But I think that this retreat might be really good for us. Ned and Fanny have also offered us marriage counseling if you're willing. I don't know how to say this…"

Looking out at his children playing without a care in the world, Rick sighed as he tried to come up with the right words. "The thing is that I have no idea how my body will respond on our wedding night. I can't promise I won't freeze or shut down."

Saying it out loud felt like stepping onto ice he wasn't sure would hold.

Marianne shifted closer, her knee brushing his. Warmth traveled through the denim, a tether pulling him back as she waited for his breath to steady.

"I'm not afraid of you," he added quickly. "Not even a little. But maybe counseling would be a good thing so we can be better prepared?"

"I'd like that." Her thumb brushed the back of his hand. "Don't forget that I will be a stereotypical virgin bride coming to you with a bundle of nerves on our wedding night. We'll just have to learn together, right?"

"Right." Rick couldn't help but smile as she kissed him.

Standing up, Marianne pulled him up to join her. "And I don't expect you to go from one hundred to zero overnight."

He blinked. "Meaning?"

"You've lived in survival mode a long time," she said. "Healing doesn't mean your body forgets how to protect itself. It means you're learning you don't have to stay braced all the time. I don't need you healed overnight. I just need you to be one hundred percent honest with me at all times, even if it's embarrassing. Okay?"

Something deep inside him unclenched as he nodded.

"You don't owe me perfection," she said, squeezing his hand. "Just honesty."

He couldn't look away.

"If you freeze, I won't think you've failed me," she said. "I'll think you trusted me enough to stay instead of shutting me out."

"I don't want to disappoint you."

"You haven't," she whispered. "You couldn't."

His shoulders eased, just a fraction. He turned toward the pond, watching the wind skim the water while Sam accused Walter of cheating loud enough for half the county to hear.

"I didn't fall in love with a fantasy husband," Marianne said. "I fell in love with the real man. The one who lets my kid sister win at cards. The one who carries my family with the same gentleness he gives his own kids."

His heart thudded, deep and grateful.

"And," she added, color rising in her cheeks, "your body is allowed to feel pleasure without fear. I'm not using your trauma as a measure of my worth."

"Marianne…"

"Yes?"

"I love you."

Her smile glowed. "I love you too."

Hand in hand they walked together toward his children and the Bertrams. Marianne twined their fingers. "I prayed for a man who saw my heart. I never expected to love someone who'd trust me with his."

Chapter Four

Text Message from Rick to Eddie

I'm here.

Eddie ran—not because he liked it, but because the walls of the house felt too tight, the air too thin, and he needed motion—something, anything—so that he wasn't sitting with the truth he still couldn't face. He took the front steps two at a time, crossed the quiet street, and headed for the coastline trail, townhomes dark and shuttered as he passed.

His breath tore from his chest in sharp bursts. Cold January air burned his lungs. His shoes slapped the pavement in a steady rhythm, a beat he could almost pretend belonged to someone who wasn't unraveling.

He ran harder, pushing himself past comfort.

If he could outrun the memory—push fast enough, far enough—maybe the guilt would quiet for a few minutes. Maybe he could catch peace the way he once caught his breath during long youth-group retreats, when exhaustion felt good and silence came easy. Maybe he could silence the question Ned had asked so calmly it still rang in his ears:

What direction are your feet turning?

Eddie didn't know, and his feet answered for him.

Santa Ana winds scraped his face raw. His heart hammered against his ribs. The trail blurred as he lengthened his stride, punishing his legs, his lungs, his body for the truth he could not smother.

But memory doesn't obey mileage, and it caught him at the halfway point—without warning, without mercy—slamming into him with the force of a physical blow.

He stumbled, a sharp inhale punching from his chest, and suddenly he wasn't on the trail anymore—he was back there.

The air carried the mingled scent of wine, citrus, and salt as the moment snapped into place—New Year's Eve, Rick's backyard, moments before midnight. String lights glowed like stars overhead, laughter spilled through the windows while the ocean churned restless and cold beyond the fence.

He should have gone home with Lucy.

He heard her again—the soft, tired *I'm heading out*, and the way she'd lingered in the hallway as if waiting for him to say, *I'll come too. You shouldn't go alone.*

He hadn't said it. He had told himself she didn't need him. That she was strong. That she'd be fine for one night. Had he been selfish to want a fun night out with their friends, without the stress and pressure of thinking about their marriage and the coming child?

He knew the answer deep in his heart but refused to put it in words as he bent to tie his shoelace.

"Pastor Ferrars?"

Looking up, Eddie immediately recognized the lanky teen who was jogging up to his side. Of all the times for someone to spot him. He wanted that invisibility clock that characters managed to create out of thin air in fantasy novels he secretly obsessed over.

"Robert, hey man, what's up?"

"Hi, Pastor, this is like such a God-thing finding you here. I've been meaning to see you before or after youth group but haven't had the guts to. I mean, it's not like I'm afraid of talking with you. I didn't mean that. It's just that…"

The kid looked so nervous hopping from one foot to another that Eddie finally took pity on him.

"What can I do for you, Robert?"

"Well, the thing is… Actually… Oh gosh, Pastor, this is so awkward."

"Sometimes it helps if you just blurt it all out instead of thinking it through too much," Eddie suggested with a slight smile.

The kid grinned and took a deep breath. "Okay, here goes. The thing is, Pastor Eddie, that I am cheating on my girlfriend Harri. Okay, maybe not physically cheating per se because I am still a virgin but emotionally yes. I hate that I am doing it but Melissa is just so fun and easy to talk with and Harri always gets all nervous and shy around me."

Looking down at his shoes, Robert Martin sighed as he kicked a pebble. "What am I supposed to do, Pastor? I don't want to tell Harri because what if she breaks up with me? And it's not like it's Melissa's fault. She's just really friendly and sweet."

"Goodness, Robert, I don't know if I'm the right person for you to talk to about this."

"But, Pastor, if not you who else would I talk to?"

Sighing as he realized just how crazy this situation had become, Eddie beckoned towards a park bench a few yards away. Eddie sank onto the bench, elbows braced on his knees, chest still heaving from the run. He gestured for Robert to sit beside him.

"Robert," he said slowly, "what makes this hard isn't that you like someone else."

The boy stiffened.

"It's that you're letting two girls hope at the same time."

Robert's shoulders sagged.

"We tell ourselves we're being kind by not choosing," Eddie said. "By compartmentalizing. Publicly, you're Harri's boyfriend. Privately, you are giving Melissa emotional space that belongs to someone else by confiding in her. Those things you tell Melissa are probably things you should be saving to tell Harri, right?"

Eddie swallowed. This was all too familiar.

"But by keeping things comfortable and the status quo we think we are protecting everyone and yet we end up hurting everyone involved."

Robert kicked at the dirt. "I didn't mean to do that."

"I know," Eddie said gently. "Most people don't."

He turned slightly, lowering his voice. "Here's the truth people don't like to say out loud: when you don't choose, you don't spare anyone pain—you divide it."

Robert frowned. "How?"

"One person starts to feel foolish for hoping," Eddie said. "The other feels guilty for wanting what isn't fully theirs. And you walk away thinking you were showing kindness and being gentle—when really, you were just afraid to take a stand."

The words landed heavier than Eddie expected. He let the silence stretch.

"So what do I do?" Robert asked at last.

"You decide who you're choosing," Eddie said. "And then you live in a way that matches that choice."

Robert nodded slowly. "And if I don't know yet?"

"Then you need to stop giving both girls something that belongs to only one," Eddie replied. "That means if you want Harri to be your girlfriend you need to respect her by not emotionally making yourself available to Melissa. Same goes for Melissa. If you respect her as a friend, you have to create boundaries so she knows you are just pals and there's no chance of it becoming something more."

The boy winced.

"And if you realize your heart isn't in it anymore," Eddie added, "then honesty is the answer. Even if it costs you one or both of the relationships."

Robert's voice dropped. "What if I lose her?"

Eddie's chest tightened, noticing the choice of pronoun and avoidance.

"That's the risk," he said quietly. "Truth doesn't promise the outcome you want or that it will be easy. It only promises that you're standing on honest ground and can respect yourself."

They sat in silence, the ocean wind threading through the low brush along the trail.

After a moment, Robert asked, "Have you ever been in a situation like that?"

Eddie didn't answer right away.

"Yes," he said at last. "And I thought I was being gentle and honorable by not cutting ties with the other woman."

He shook his head once.

"I wasn't. I was letting her hope for something I already knew wasn't even an option."

Robert nodded, eyes fixed on the pavement. "I think… I think I know what I need to do."

"I'm glad to hear that," Eddie said, standing. "The fact you are even thinking about this is respectable and takes more courage than you realize."

Robert gave a small, nervous smile. "Thanks, Pastor. I guess you'll know how it goes when you see me on Sunday."

Eddie smiled and shook the boy's hand as they parted ways with a promise to pray for him.

As the boy jogged back down the trail, Eddie remained where he was, breath steadying at last.

The question Ned had asked returned—quiet, unyielding.

What direction are your feet turning?

Eddie looked down the path that led home.

He straightened and forced himself to walk, feet heavy against the path. He hadn't reached for Elinor. Hadn't spoken the words she wanted to fan the flame of hope. But he'd let the moment linger. He had let her hope breathe when it should have been named and buried.

He glanced to his left as he started to make his way home, watching waves crash and retreat, relentless and indifferent. The sea didn't care that he was a pastor. It didn't care about vows or titles or intentions. It moved forward, doing exactly what it was made to do.

He wished he were that honest.

By the time he reached the street, his legs trembled with exhaustion. His house came into view, windows dark and still.

Lucy's car was gone.

The absence hit harder than he expected.

Inside, the house felt hollow.

He dropped his keys on the counter and stood there, listening to the refrigerator hum and the clock ticking toward a future he had endangered.

He moved through the rooms slowly, looking for something he couldn't name. He passed the living room couch where Lucy slept when nausea overtook her. The bathroom where she'd knelt, palms braced against the tile, this morning as sickness washed over her. The spare room with its bright color swatches of paint on the wall waiting for a decision.

Finally, he stopped in the doorway of their bedroom.

Her pillow remained indented. Her scent of clean soap, strawberries, and something soft and familiar lingered faintly. He lay down on her side of the bed and pressed his face into her pillow, inhaling her scent and letting himself cry.

Drying his eyes, he pulled out his phone, opened his messages, and scrolled. His fingers hovered, then moved with purpose.

We need to talk today. I owe you honesty.

He stared at the words, heart pounding, then sent it before fear could argue him out of it.

The house stayed silent.

Eddie lay back on the bed, one arm thrown over his eyes, breath slowing as exhaustion finally claimed him. He didn't know what Lucy would say. He didn't know if courage would be enough to save what he'd damaged.

But for the first time in days, he wasn't running, and that, he hoped as exhaustion finally claimed him, would be enough for today.

Chapter Five

Rick's Journal

I am learning to see the world at the pace my daughter needs, not the speed my fear prefers.

Ellie bounced on her toes like a rubber ball ready to pop. "Are we leaving yet?"

"It's been two minutes since you last asked," Rick said as he tied his sneakers.

"That's a long time."

"To whom?"

"Me and Flippers."

The stuffed penguin stared at him from her backpack like a silent accomplice. Shaking his head in mock exasperation, Rick checked his backpack one last time—snacks, water bottles, emergency pull-ups ("for Flippers," Ellie insisted, "just in case"), and his camera.

"Are you sure you don't want to bring Quackers with you today?"

"Nah." Ellie patted Quackers on the head. "He's keeping Mr. Knightley company."

As soon as their neighbor George Knightley arrived for babysitting duty with coffee in one hand and the newest paperback thriller in

the other, Ellie scrambled over, gave him a fierce hug, then spun
back to Rick. "Can we go now? Please?"

"All right." Rick grinned. "Let our daddy daughter date time
begin."

Ellie cheered, then immediately whispered, "Shhh." She pressed a
finger to her lips.

"Why are we shushing?"

She pointed upstairs. "The boys and Lily are still asleep."

His chest warmed. He loved how she was always thinking of
others, even at three years of age. He scooped her up and kissed
her cheek.

"We'll be quiet like mice."

"Flippers is not a mouse," she corrected gravely, leaning her
forehead against his. "It's a good day, Daddy."

Something in him settled. "Yeah," he whispered. "It really is."

They reached the car without waking anyone, which in itself was an
accomplishment worthy of medals. The Saturday morning air was
chilly but bright, and Ellie narrated everything out the window as
he drove toward the freeway.

"Look! A dog. Look! Two dogs. Look! A dog in a stroller. Daddy,
that dog has a jacket."

"California dogs are fancy."

She nodded solemnly. "Daniel's going to want a jacket."

Rick smiled. If Daniel wanted to be a jacket dog, then Daniel would be a jacket dog, no questions asked.

The aquarium parking lot was mostly empty when he pulled in. After paying for their admission, he let Ellie skip every third step just to hear her giggle as they made their way around the first room.

"Penguins!" Ellie cried, pointing at a picture on the wall. "Flippers was born here."

"Born?" he echoed, amused.

"Wasn't he?"

He'd bought Flippers at the zoo last year, but stuffed-animal origin stories apparently could be changed at the drop of a hat. He let it go.

Ellie pressed her nose to the glass of the central tank. "Hello, friends," she whispered.

Rick watched her face. He didn't miss the way she leaned into his leg without looking. Even though she'd been days shy of her second birthday when Louisa had taken her from his arms, he knew she carried her own scars from that season. His therapist had said just this last week that some fears lived in the body long after memory faded, and he would give anything to lift every trace of fear from his children.

"Daddy, can we find the penguins?" Ellie tugged on his pant leg. "Flippers wants to say hi."

"Lead the way."

She marched ahead, backpack bouncing, but glanced back every few steps to make sure he was still there. She didn't remember the cellar. But he could tell that her body remembered separation just as much as his heart remembered her screams as Louisa took her upstairs on Thanksgiving.

In the penguin hall, Ellie pressed Flippers to the glass. "He missed you," she informed a confused penguin who was swimming in circles. Rick stood behind her, hands resting lightly on her shoulders.

Marianne had once told him healing often looked like ordinary Tuesdays. Maybe it looked like this, too—the hush of water, soft lighting, and a little girl who kept checking to make sure her father hadn't vanished.

After exploring everything Ellie wanted, they shared a basket of overpriced chicken tenders and fries. Ellie arranged each fry with care, dipping them into exactly four ketchup dots, and insisted Rick eat Flippers' portion.

Mid-bite, she paused. Her brow pinched. "Daddy, what's a retreat?"

Rick blinked. "Where did you hear that?"

"Lily says Uncle Darcy and Aunt Caroline are going on one. And she said you are too." She lowered her voice. "Are you?"

He chose his words carefully. "Yes. After the wedding, Pastors Fanny and Ned are giving Miss Marianne and me a gift. They're going to take us on a trip. It's going to be a time for us grown-ups with God and with each other."

Ellie considered that, fingers curling around Flippers' wing. "Will you come back?"

The question landed like a bruise being pressed.

Rick leaned closer. "Absolutely," he said. "I'll come back, Little Love. And honestly? You're going to have so much fun while we're away that you won't even miss me. You know you get to stay with Aunt Caroline and Uncle Darcy for a full two weeks and then Mr. Knightley is coming over to stay for a week."

Her shoulders loosened. "Okay. Can you bring me a bear like in my book?"

"You drive a hard bargain."

On the drive home, Ellie fell asleep clutching Flippers, a contented smile on her face. Rick watched her in the rearview mirror.

One day she'd be tall like her mother. One day she'd outgrow stuffed animals. One day she might stop clinging to his sleeve when he stepped too far away.

But today, she trusted him with her whole world.

At a stoplight, his phone buzzed. The notification flashed on the car display.

Missed call: Eddie Ferrars.

Rick frowned. He'd texted twice this week with simple invitations for coffee and conversation and received no response.

A missed call with no voicemail was worse. He recognized the pattern instantly. Shame never announced itself cleanly. It delayed.

Hid. He'd lived it himself—months ago, bristling when Darcy nudged him toward help.

He pulled into the driveway and shut off the engine. Ellie slept on, mouth parted, grip tight on Flippers. Rick sat for a moment, hand resting on the wheel, holding two truths at once.

He was wildly, undeservingly blessed. And each day he felt himself easing closer to the kind of honesty Marianne and his children quietly drew out of him.

But one of his closest friends was drowning across town and pretending he wasn't.

Rick whispered a prayer. "Please be with Eddie and Lucy, Father."

Ellie stirred, blinking awake. "Daddy?"

"Yeah, Little Love?"

She rubbed her eyes, breath catching. "You didn't disappear."

His heart twisted. "No," he said softly. "Never."

"Okay." She leaned toward him, arms out, trusting. "I love you."

It undid him every time.

Rick smiled, throat tight. "Love you more."

And he meant it. With every part of who he was, who he had been, and the man he was still becoming, he held her close.

Staying, he realized, was only brave if he was willing to risk leaving—and trust that love would not disappear the moment he loosened his grip.

Rick kissed Ellie's hair and carried her inside, grateful for the quiet courage it took to stay present when fear begged him to lock every door.

Chapter Six

Eddie stood in the crackers aisle longer than necessary, staring at a shelf of brightly colored boxes and shaking his head at the sheer number of choices.

He had come armed with a shopping list written in Lucy's looping handwriting and good intentions. Grocery shopping was the least he could do, and it felt good, in a hollow sort of way, to be useful.

Now, though, as he reached for a box of saltines, he felt embarrassingly ill-equipped for such a simple task. Who knew there were so many variations? He considered calling Lucy, then stopped himself. If she was finally asleep, the last thing he wanted to do was wake her.

Mr. Cole's grocery store was busy for a weekday morning—retirees, young mothers with toddlers, and the odd man here or there like himself. He had chosen the early hour deliberately, but he had underestimated Croft Beach's residents.

"Pastor Ferrars?"

The voice was soft, musical and undeniably recognizable. Eddie closed his eyes for half a second before turning.

The associate pastor's wife, Mrs. Collins, stood at the end of the aisle with a basket looped casually over her arm, two other women flanking her like parentheses. All three wore variations of the same uniform: pressed blouses, tailored slacks, tasteful jewelry, and hair blow-dried with care, likely just done at the beauty salon.

"Hello, ladies," Eddie said, managing a smile.

"Well, goodness," Mrs. Collins said a touch too loudly. "We were just saying how much we missed seeing you in the pulpit on Sunday. Are you all right?"

The question was gentle. The interest was not.

"I'm fine," Eddie said. "Just running errands."

One of the women glanced at his basket. "Oh, that's kind. Lucy not feeling well?"

His chest tightened.

"She's tired," he said carefully. "Thank you for asking."

"Of course." Mrs. Collins nodded, lips pursed sympathetically. "Lucy tried so hard with the nativity, didn't she?"

Eddie's jaw tightened.

"Those productions can be… a lot for some women," she continued smoothly. "Not everyone takes to that kind of visible leadership naturally. And I am sure it is harder since she has not yet been blessed with the gift of motherhood."

At the mention of motherhood, something dark and protective flared in Eddie's chest. If only they knew that Lucy was carrying their child.

"If she wants help next year," Mrs. Collins went on, "I would be happy to add it to my schedule, along with my other committees."

"It was such a shame your beautiful daughter was not Mary again this year," one of the women added. "You really should try to explain how things are done around here to your wife, Pastor."

Eddie bit the inside of his cheek.

"She gave it everything she had," he insisted. "I thought it was one of the best nativity plays Croft Beach Community Church has ever had."

"Yes," Mrs. Collins conceded. "She did try."

"Yes," Eddie said evenly. "I will let her know."

Thinking the conversation was pointless and going nowhere, Eddie turned his cart as if to leave when Mrs. Collins tilted her head.

"I also heard you are taking a sabbatical."

The word landed heavily.

"It will not be long," Eddie said, keeping his voice steady. "I just needed some time at home."

"Oh, of course," one of the women murmured. "Burnout is so common."

"So common," Mrs. Collins agreed. "Especially when a man stretches himself thin."

She lowered her voice. "The board has been praying fervently. These are delicate times. Stability matters."

"I am grateful for their support," Eddie said through clenched teeth. "As for Lucy? She is exactly who I want beside me. I could not have asked for a better wife."

Mrs. Collins smiled, her eyes sharp. "I am sure."

"I should finish my shopping," he said, already pushing the cart forward. "Lucy is waiting."

"Of course," Mrs. Collins replied. "We will be praying."

He nodded once more and turned into the dairy aisle, his breath coming faster now, his chest tight with something uncomfortably close to panic.

And then he saw Elinor.

She stood near the yogurt case, phone wedged between her shoulder and ear, scanning labels.

"Yes, Marianne," she said softly. "Low-fat or full? What? Oh dear. I will grab both."

She laughed in an unguarded moment and Eddie saw before him the carefree young woman he'd once known in college. She'd been so easy to talk to.

Looking down, Eddie was appalled and frightened to see that his cart had already angled toward her as if on autopilot. It would be so easy to talk to her. Elinor was always kind. Always willing to listen. But that was the problem he'd got himself into in December.

She shifted the phone from her shoulder and looked up.

His cart bumped lightly against the shelf as he rushed to turn away, the sound louder than it should have been. He pushed down the next aisle without looking back.

By the time he reached the checkout, his chest felt heavy. He loaded the items onto the conveyor belt and realized too late that he had forgotten the ginger tea Lucy liked best.

"Find everything you needed?" the cashier asked.

"Yes," Eddie lied.

Outside, the sun felt too bright. He placed the groceries in the trunk without care, closed it, and stood there with his keys dangling uselessly in his hand.

He thought of Lucy at home. Of her hand finding his in the dark. Of Mrs. Collins' smile. Of Elinor's laugh. Of the pulpit he was stepping away from.

He was not ready to go home.

The thought of Lucy's hopeful smile—of how little he felt he deserved it—made his chest ache.

Eddie slid into the driver's seat and shut the door, gripping the steering wheel until his knuckles whitened.

"I am supposed to be better than this," he whispered.

And being better, he realized with a dull ache settling in his chest, would mean refusing to let silence do any more damage—no more half-truths, no more unspoken hope, and no more letting anyone believe he was still undecided.

CHAPTER SEVEN

Rick hadn't planned to make the call that afternoon.

But once he'd walked through the door and found George Knightley reading aloud Lily's favorite Bible story of Daniel and the lions' den in his calm, baritone voice with the kids and Daniel the dog laying around the den in rapture, Rick quietly slid Ellie to the floor and walked into the kitchen in search of a cup of coffee but instead pulled out his phone.

He scrolled to Ned's name and hit dial before he could talk himself out of it.

"Rick," Ned answered after the second ring. "Everything okay?"

Rick swallowed. "I think it could be. I just… I think I need help making sure it is."

There was a pause as Rick listened to Ned breathing on the other end of the line.

"Do you want to come by?" Ned asked.

Rick glanced toward the den, where Ellie's laugh floated down the hall. "Would you be willing to come here instead? The kids are home."

"Of course," Ned said. "Fanny and I can be there in ten minutes."

Ten minutes later, after saying goodbye to George, Rick closed the front door and looked at Marianne and the Bertrams where they sat comfortably in the front room.

The muffled sound of children arguing over a board game drifted in from the den.

"This doesn't need to be formal," Fanny said gently, relaxing back into the armchair. "We're just talking."

Rick nodded, hands clasped together, foot tapping once before he forced it still. Marianne held out her hand and he went to sit beside her. She didn't rush him. She never did.

Ned leaned forward slightly. "What made you call today?"

Rick exhaled slowly. "Ellie asked me if I was coming back when the honeymoon and retreat were brought up."

Marianne's hand tightened in his.

"I told her yes," Rick continued. "And I meant it. But I realized something on the drive home." His voice roughened. "I don't want to promise presence and then carry fear into our marriage like it's baggage we're supposed to ignore."

Fanny nodded. "That's wise."

Rick hesitated, then spoke carefully. "When I say I want to feel safe… I don't mean comfortable."

Ned waited.

"It means choice," Rick said quietly. "It means having the freedom to hit the stop button. I know nothing will happen to me without my consent when I'm with Marianne however I don't think my body knows that."

Marianne turned fully toward him. "I'm glad you know it, though," she said without hesitation.

Rick looked at her, searching her face. She didn't flinch.

Fanny smiled softly. "That's not fear speaking," she said. "That's wisdom shaped by survival."

Rick let out a breath he hadn't realized he was holding.

"I don't want our wedding night to feel like something I have to get through," he admitted. "I want it to feel like something we're choosing. Together."

Suddenly the room felt much too warm. The edges of Rick's vision softened, light blurring at the corners.

He shifted his weight, grounding his feet against the rug. The den door down the hall creaked. A child laughed.

His pulse spiked anyway.

Marianne noticed immediately and angled her body towards Rick so he could see her. "I've got you, Rick."

Rick breathed in through his nose. Out through his mouth.

Ned and Fanny waited. No one rushed him.

The moment passed, but as always it left its mark.

"This," Rick said when he could speak again, voice rough. "This is why I called."

Ned nodded. "Then here's the truth," he said. "Intimacy isn't a test of courage. It's a conversation. And conversations move at the pace of the slowest nervous system in the room."

Marianne grinned as she elbowed Rick in the ribs playfully. "That would be Rick's," she said. "I'm learning how to slow down, on the other hand."

Rick huffed out a breath that was almost a laugh.

Fanny leaned forward. "There is no timeline you have to meet. No expectation you have to fulfill. Don't feel ready to consummate your wedding on your wedding night? That's okay too. Your only responsibility is honesty with yourself and with each other."

Rick nodded, emotion pressing hard against his ribs.

"So if I freeze," he asked quietly, "that doesn't mean I've failed?"

"It means your body is asking for gentleness," Fanny replied. "And gentleness is not failure."

From the den came a shout as Walter accused Lily of cheating.

Marianne squeezed Rick's hand. "See?" she murmured. "Real life."

Rick smiled, something in him easing.

From the den, Ellie's voice rose clear and bright. "Daddy! Lily won!"

Grinning at the other adults, Rick shouted, "Congratulations, Sweetheart!"

Fanny rose with a chuckle. "Sounds like our cue to say goodnight," she said with a wink.

Marianne laughed softly and stood with her. She leaned down and pressed a quick kiss to Rick's temple. "I'll be right back."

Rick nodded, watching as the two women disappeared down the hall, their voices lowering instinctively as they neared the den.

The house settled into a quieter stillness.

Rick remained seated, elbows resting on his knees, fingers laced together. Ned didn't rush him. He never did.

After a moment, Rick spoke.

"Can I ask you something without you trying to fix it?"

Ned leaned back in his chair. "You usually do."

Rick huffed out a breath, then sobered. "What if I'm rushing this?"

Ned tilted his head slightly. "What do you mean by *this*?"

Rick stared at the floor. "The wedding. The retreat. The idea that I'm supposed to be ready for something my body still flinches away from." His voice dropped. "What if more time would make it easier?"

Ned didn't answer right away.

Instead, he asked quietly, "When do you think it wouldn't feel rushed?"

Rick opened his mouth — then closed it.

The answer rose immediately, unwelcome and undeniable.

"It wouldn't matter," he admitted. "Six months. A year. Five years." He shook his head once. "My body wouldn't suddenly forget. The fear would still show up."

Ned nodded. "That's what I thought."

Rick glanced up. "So what am I supposed to do with that?"

"You stop using time as a way to negotiate with fear," Ned said gently. "Fear always asks for more."

Rick swallowed.

"Readiness," Ned continued, "isn't about the absence of fear. It's about the presence of trust."

Rick let that settle.

"I trust Marianne," he said slowly. "Completely."

"I know," Ned said. "That's why Fanny and I support you both wholeheartedly and why you're here now instead of years from now."

Rick leaned back, the weight of it pressing in with clarity.

"So I'm not reckless?" he murmured to himself. "I'm just… realistic."

Ned smiled faintly. "You're choosing to live instead of waiting to feel safe enough to begin."

Footsteps approached, soft and familiar. Marianne reappeared in the doorway, her expression warm and tired in the best way.

"All tucked in," she said quietly. "They insisted on two bedtime stories tonight."

Rick smiled up at this beautiful woman who was taking on not just him and his nightmares but also his three children.

Ned stood with a chuckle. "Well, I'll see you both on Sunday," he said. Then, more softly, "You're not rushing, Rick. You're listening. Keep doing what you're doing."

Rick walked the Bertrams to the door and stood there for a moment after it closed, taking a moment to appreciate the peace.

Marianne slipped her hand into his.

"Better?" she asked.

Rick nodded. "Yeah. I think so."

The fear wasn't gone, but he finally understood it wasn't in charge of the clock.

CHAPTER EIGHT

Eddie came home to the quiet hum of the dishwasher and the faint glow of the kitchen light left on deliberately, as if Lucy had wanted the house to feel less empty when he walked through the door.

She stood at the counter, one hand braced against the edge, the other absently rubbing her stomach as she stared at the sink. Her hair was pulled back loosely, face pale in a way that still startled him when he noticed it.

"You're late," she said without turning around.

"I stopped by the Bertrams' house," Eddie replied, setting his keys down carefully. "I needed to—"

She turned then, her expression composed but tight. "I know."

The words landed harder than he expected.

"You know?" he repeated.

"I ran into Fanny at the pharmacy," Lucy said. "She mentioned Ned is preaching again this Sunday."

Eddie's stomach dropped.

"And then," she continued evenly, "Mrs. Collins texted to say how grateful she is that you're taking a few weeks off to rest."

Eddie opened his mouth. Closed it.

Lucy watched him closely. "So yes," she said. "I know."

"I didn't mean for you to hear it that way," Eddie said quickly. "I was going to tell you."

"But you didn't," Lucy bit out.

The space between them thickened.

"I needed guidance," Eddie said. "I was drowning, Lucy. I didn't know what to do."

"I understand that," she said softly. "What I don't understand is why Pastor Ned heard about it before I did."

The words were quiet. They cut anyway.

"I didn't tell him everything," Eddie said. "I just—"

"You told him enough," Lucy interrupted, not quite raising her voice. "Enough that the board knows you're stepping back. Enough that people are praying. Enough that our marriage is suddenly a topic for speculation."

"That's not fair," Eddie said, heat rising despite himself. "I asked for help."

"And I'm glad you did," Lucy said. "But you asked *him* before you asked *me.*"

Eddie ran a hand through his hair. "I didn't want to burden you."

Lucy let out a breath that trembled. "I wear your wedding ring, Edward Robert Ferrars," she said quietly. "I am already bearing this with my body every day by carrying your baby. You don't get to decide what burdens me."

The truth of it stole his breath.

"I was trying to protect you," he said, weaker now.

"Protection without honesty feels like a pat on the back," Lucy replied. "And that's something we could really use right now. Honesty. Look, I know that I ran off on New Year's Day and haven't been the most cheerful and chatty of Cathys but at least I haven't gone around telling every Tracy, Diana, and Helen I run into about our marriage!"

Silence stretched between them, filled with the low hum of appliances and the ticking of the clock over the stove.

"I told him about the kiss," Eddie admitted.

Lucy's eyes closed.

"Not all of it," he rushed on. "But enough. I needed someone to tell me what was right."

Lucy opened her eyes again. "What was right? Do you honestly not know that it was wrong to kiss Elinor?"

"For goodness sake! I didn't kiss her. She kissed me!"

"Semantics!" Lucy cried out as she turned away to look out the window.

"And how many people know now?" she asked, as she turned back around to look at him with suspiciously red eyes.

"Ned," Eddie said. "Fanny, probably. The elders know I'm stepping back but I swear I didn't tell them about us but just that I needed some rest."

"And me," Lucy said. "Eventually."

The word stung.

Eddie swallowed. "Maybe we should just tell everyone," he said suddenly. "About the baby. About us. Bring everything into the light."

Lucy stared at him.

"Is that what you want," she asked carefully, "or is that what feels easier than sitting in this moment?"

Eddie faltered.

"I want to be honest," he said.

"Even with me?"

Her hand rested protectively over her stomach again. Eddie noticed the gesture, how instinctive it was, and felt the sharp twist of guilt that followed.

"I don't know how to fix this," he said, voice breaking.

Lucy's shoulders slumped, the first visible crack in her composure.

"I am not asking you to fix everything overnight or to backpedal and undo what you've done with Elinor," she sighed. "I am however asking you to stay."

The words lodged in his chest.

He nodded, unable to trust himself to speak.

"I need some air," he said after a moment. "I'm going to go for a run."

Lucy didn't argue. She didn't follow him to the door. She simply nodded once.

"Don't be long," she said.

"I won't," Eddie automatically replied as the night air hit him hard as he stepped outside. He jogged without stretching, lungs burning almost immediately as he pushed himself down the street, past familiar houses and darkened windows.

Running usually helped.

Tonight, it didn't.

When he slowed, chest heaving, he realized he had circled back to the house. Instead of walking up to the front door however, he kept going. His feet carried him to the car.

He opened the trunk and stared at the overnight bag tucked neatly in the corner. He hadn't used the bag in years and yet it was a habit from years of late hospital calls and emergency counseling sessions to always be prepared.

He told himself this was no different.

Just one night wouldn't hurt anyone. He felt sure space to think and pray what exactly what he needed.

Slamming the trunk closed, he slid behind the wheel and drove until he spotted a hotel sign glowing in the dark.

At the front desk, he gave his name, accepted the key card, and climbed the stairs without looking back.

By the time he closed the door behind him, the truth pressed in with quiet clarity:

He hadn't chosen rest.

He had chosen distance.

And he didn't know how many more nights that choice would cost him.

CHAPTER NINE

Rick cut the engine and glanced at the kids in the rearview mirror.

Ellie, secure in her car seat, had Quackers tucked firmly under one arm like a boarding pass she refused to surrender. Lily sat beside her, calm and observant, her gaze already fixed on the house ahead. In the middle row, Walter and Sam were deep in animated debate about a video game they had been obsessed with ever since spending the night at their friend Noah's.

"We're early, Little Love," Rick said as he watched Ellie impatiently tug at her straps.

Ellie beamed. "Aunt Caroline is waiting."

Rick smiled and opened his door and immediately got to work releasing his youngest from her car seat as the others jumped out of the SUV.

The front door swung open before they reached it.

"There's my little girl," Caroline said warmly, as Ellie bolted forward, sandals slapping against the walkway. Caroline caught her easily, settling her against her hip as if they had always belonged that way.

"I brought Quackers," Ellie announced solemnly, pressing the duck between them.

"Excellent," Caroline replied gravely. "I was worried he'd miss everything important."

Ellie giggled, already home.

Rick lingered a moment longer, Lily at his side, as Walter and Sam jogged up behind them, telling Caroline their over-the-top suggestions for what improvements she could do as principal at their school.

"A video game room in the computer room?" Caroline asked, with a hint of amusement in her voice. "And here I thought we already had games on the computers."

"Not the cool ones," Sam corrected. "Oregon Trail is so oldddddd."

"Hey, don't knock The Oregon Trail," Darcy interrupted good naturedly. That was my jam when I was your age."

"Hi, Uncle Darcy," Lily greeted him with a hug and whispered, "Don't worry. I like to play too."

Rick stepped inside, feeling much at home as he watched his kids scatter. This house had held the Wentworths for eight months—long enough to feel like home, even now.

They gathered in the living room as afternoon light streamed through the windows. Caroline set Ellie down on the couch, where she immediately bounced into the cushions. Walter and Sam sprawled on the floor, as they studied the latest crossword puzzle Caroline had clipped from the back of a magazine. Lily settled beside Rick, thumbing through the magazine.

"So," Caroline said, perching on the arm of the chair beside Darcy, "we promised pictures."

Darcy snorted. "You promised. I was overruled."

"Want to see our honeymoon photos?" Caroline asked the kids. "We went all over Europe. Italy. London. Paris."

Ellie gasped. "That's a lot of walking."

Rick laughed quietly.

Caroline connected her phone to the television and began swiping through photos. Darcy stood in front of the Colosseum. Caroline laughed in the rain outside a Paris bookshop. There were videos of the two of them, windblown and unguarded, riding a vespa through narrow streets and even riding in a hot air balloon. The kids leaned in, reacting loudly. Sam and Lily rated the photos on a scale of one to five. Walter asked how many steps they had walked. Ellie tried to hug the screen every time Caroline appeared.

Rick's chest filled with gratitude he knew he could never repay. Darcy had not just given them shelter. He had given them their lives back.

When the last photo had been admired, Caroline turned off the television.

"Rick," she said, casual but deliberate, "there's something I wanted to talk to you about."

He straightened.

"I officially stepped into the lower school principal role last week," she continued. "That means I'm involved in staffing decisions."

Darcy shifted beside her, his shoulders tightening as if he knew where the conversation was headed.

"There's a science teaching position opening up after Easter," Caroline said. "Marine science is part of the curriculum."

Rick blinked. "You're serious? Mr. Perry's class?"

"I am serious and yes, Mr. Perry is retiring early due to a family emergency which means he'll have to move out of the country."

"I don't have a credential," he said automatically.

"Jane Austen Academy is a private school," she replied. "You have the science degree. And you know how to teach kids."

Rick glanced instinctively at his children.

"I work part-time at Darcy's firm," he said slowly.

Darcy exhaled. "Yes. You do." He hesitated. "And I primarily hired you because I wanted you close and because you needed something that wasn't therapy or survival."

Rick absorbed that.

"But the filing backlog is gone," Darcy continued. "And I don't need you there anymore." He met Rick's eyes. "This would actually give me room to hire someone else."

The room went quiet.

"This isn't charity," Caroline said gently. "It's a job."

Ellie slid off the couch and toddled over, arms raised. Rick lifted her without thinking.

"Daddy go to school?" she asked.

"Maybe, Little Love."

Lily leaned closer. "You're the best."

The truth of that settled somewhere deep.

"Think about it," Caroline said.

Rick did.

A couple days later, the science room smelled faintly of saltwater and rubbing alcohol. Rick was surprised by how much came back the moment he stepped inside after nearly fifteen years. The long lab tables bore the marks of careful use. Posters of tide pools and marine ecosystems lined one wall, sun-faded at the edges, while other walls held biology and chemistry posters.

A small aquarium bubbled near the window, a lone hermit crab inching along the glass.

"I always meant to upgrade the tank," Mr. Perry said with a rueful smile as he dropped in pieces of fruit. "Never quite got around to it."

"If that's the same hermit crab from when I was a student, I'm impressed," Rick said. "Keeping it alive counts."

Mr. Perry studied him, then smiled. "I should have recognized you sooner. I was distracted by the idea that you were standing on the responsible side of the room again."

Rick laughed softly.

They caught up laughing over remembered stories of Darcy playing pranks in the classroom. Caroline laughed, jingling her braids, as she listened in rapture to a tale of Darcy putting a paper machete mask of the former principal's face into a jug of water on April Fool's Day.

As their allotted hour came to a close, the humor softened into something steadier.

"You always paid attention," Mr. Perry said at last. "Even when you were getting into trouble with that pal of yours."

Rick swallowed.

"I would be honored to pass this classroom on to you," Mr. Perry said.

The room felt smaller suddenly, the ceiling pressing lower. Rick drew in a breath that did not go all the way down and stepped back, grounding himself until the walls settled again.

"I'm scared," he said quietly.

No one rushed to answer him.

Charlotte, the upper school principal, finally spoke up from the back of the room where'd she been quietly observing the reunion. "That doesn't concern me," she said. "It tells me you care and want to do your best."

An hour later, Rick signed his name along the line.

The pen scratched across the paper, solid and final. For the first time since the cellar, he would be able to support his family without borrowing mercy from a friend and the weight of that responsibility felt right as he smiled up at Charlotte and Caroline.

Rick thanked Charlotte as he stepped out of the upper school office, and followed Caroline down the exterior walkway toward the lower campus, where he had parked his car.

"Daddy!"

Lily reached him first, soccer ball tucked under one arm. Sam and Walter skidded to a stop beside her.

"Guess who'll be teaching here after Easter?"

Laughing at their incredulous expressions, Rick smiled. "Your old man, that's who."

There was a beat of silence, then complete chaos, which was only halted by the bell.

As his children ran back to their classrooms, Rick stood still for a moment allowing the joy to settle in his chest.

As soon as he was back in his car, he pulled out his phone, and immediately began to dial Marianne, his heart pounding as he imagined the sound of her pride.

Chapter Ten

Eddie told himself that he was not hiding or running.

The phone lay faceup on the nightstand, lighting the mundane brown hotel room in brief pulses as the screen dimmed and brightened again. He had not turned it off or even bothered to silence it. Some part of him wanted it there as proof that someone still expected something from him, even if he could not bring himself to answer.

His overnight bag lay half-zipped on the other bed, exactly where he had dropped it the night before. He had not unpacked. The brown walled room, with the strong scent of industrial cleaner, the old carpet that looked like it should have been binned years ago, and the thin curtains that failed to keep out the light and sound from the parking lot, offered no explanation for why he had stayed in a two-star hotel one town over.

He had slept maybe two hours.

Every time he closed his eyes, Lucy's face appeared. He could picture Lucy sitting alone at the kitchen table looking at his empty seat with a mixture of anger and disappointment. It was the imagined disappointment that broke him each time, and he could not seem to get ahead of it no matter what idea he came up with. It was not as though he could ask Elinor to leave town.

He should go home. His chest tightened at the thought.

He swung his legs off the bed and let his feet sink into the thin carpet. Eddie still wasn't ready to answer Ned's question, feeling lucky that he had at least managed to drag his feet out of bed for the morning. Taking a deep breath, he showered, dressed, checked out, and drove home on muscle memory alone.

Traffic lights blurred. Familiar streets passed without a blink of the eye. He rehearsed opening lines during the drive but none survived long enough to reach the driveway. Each version of his greeting collapsed the moment he imagined Lucy's face receiving it.

Her car was in the driveway. The kitchen light was on.

His chest tightened as he parked, keys heavy in his hand. He sat for a moment longer than necessary, wondering if this emotion he felt was happiness she was home or fear of how things would transpire, then forced himself out of the car and up the walk. He unlocked the door and stepped inside.

Lucy stood in the kitchen, barefoot in sweatpants and one of his old college shirts, stirring eggs at the stove. Steam curled around her face, catching in her hair.

For one foolish second, he let himself imagine that nothing had happened. That it was an ordinary morning and he was coming in from a run, not from a hotel down the freeway because he could not face how deeply he had hurt her.

"Morning," he said quietly, dropping his overnight bag by the door with a thud.

She did not jump or flinch. She stirred once more, steady and unhurried, before speaking.

"You didn't come home after your run."

"I know," he said. "I'm sorry. I just—"

"I made enough for two," she said, nodding toward the pot. "I wasn't sure when—or if—you'd be coming back."

She had made oatmeal. It was such an ordinary breakfast – the kind that married people ate on a typical morning yet nothing about today felt ordinary or typical to Eddie. Nothing about it felt steady.

He sat automatically when she set a bowl in front of him. She served herself another and took the chair across from him, leaving space between their knees. After a stilted prayer, they ate quietly. The scrape of spoons and the soft clink of ceramic sounded louder than it should have but with a limited arsenal of words Eddie focused on eating.

Watching Lucy across the table, Eddie saw her hand as it rested protectively over her stomach, full of hope, and the sight twisted something sharp in his chest.

"Would you like for us to tell people soon?" he asked, the question escaping before he had fully thought it through.

Her hand stilled. She did not lift her eyes.

"Rick and Darcy know," she murmured. "Caroline and Marianne too. Don't you remember telling them?"

He nodded. "Right. Of course."

"But if you want to tell the congregation—and Elinor—I'm okay with that," she added gently.

The way she named Elinor so plainly unsettled him. Eddie nodded and took another bite, aware that any response would only deepen the water.

She ate another spoonful, then asked, "Did you talk to Pastor Ned?"

"Not since yesterday," Eddie admitted. "People seem happy to see him back in the pulpit, don't they?"

"That's nice." She nodded once. "And are you going to keep talking to him about us?"

"If he's willing and you don't mind my doing so," Eddie said. "Yes."

Something eased in her shoulders as she nodded her consent. He saw it and felt both grateful and ashamed for how little it took to make her happy.

They ate in silence another minute before Lucy set down her spoon.

"I need to ask something," she said quietly. "And I need you to tell me the absolute truth."

His stomach clenched but he looked up to her and saw her lip tremble.

"Do you still want this marriage?"

The answer burbled instinctively inside him. "Yes."

She studied him, the careful gaze of someone trying to see whether the fracture ran all the way through.

"Then I will fight for us too," she said, her voice soft but unwavering.

His throat tightened. "Lucy—"

"But I will not fight alone," she continued. "And I will not fight whatever you are hiding."

There it was.

"She kissed me," he said.

Lucy did not flinch. She already knew that part.

"But that isn't what's eating me alive," he confessed. His breath came shallow. "The worst part is that I didn't stop her fast enough."

The silence settled between them, heavy and unyielding.

"I should have set boundaries when she first arrived," he said. "I let things go further than they ever should have."

Lucy closed her eyes for three seconds. When she opened them, her voice trembled.

"Thank you," she said. "For saying that."

Something inside him splintered.

Her fingers brushed her stomach again. "It matters," she whispered. "More than ever."

He felt the pull to say more, to empty everything he had been carrying since New Year's, but he knew he was not ready to survive the fall that would follow when the floorboard was pulled out from underneath him.

"Will you be home tonight?" she asked.

"Yes," he said instantly. "I will. I promise."

She nodded and stood to rinse her bowl. She did not ask where he had slept or demand his phone. She carried her grief with a quiet dignity that made him feel unworthy to remain in the room.

He finished eating slowly, staring at his hands long after the bowl was empty. He set it beside hers in the sink and paused.

"I do love you," he said softly.

Her chin trembled. "I know," she whispered. "I'm trying to believe it again."

He left before she could see the tears burning behind his eyes.

He sat in his parked car for a long time, hands useless on the steering wheel.

He did not know where he was going yet, but he knew two things: he was no longer behind a pulpit, and he was running out of places to hide.

Chapter Eleven

They arrived late to church thanks to a misplaced shoe that had somehow ended up in the laundry basket. Rick hustled the kids through check-in, greeted volunteers and friends as the older kids raced off toward their classrooms, waving over their shoulders. Just as quickly, he handed Ellie off to her preschool teacher, Harri Smith, before heading for the sanctuary.

Entering the sanctuary mid-song, Rick scanned the room and spotted Marianne toward the front. She was with her sisters, Maggie and Elinor, in the middle of a row already filled on both sides, leaving no open seat beside them.

Elinor's posture was composed, her hands folded neatly in her lap, but there was a tension Rick could not quite name in the tight way she held her back rigid. She did not turn when Rick slipped into an empty spot next to Mr. Cole, though Maggie and Marianne did, offering him big smiles before facing forward again.

"You look tired," the jovial supermarket owner said with a wink. "Have the kids been keeping you up?"

"You should know," Rick chuckled, thinking of the man's six children. The Cole family could easily field a volleyball team without outside help.

As Pastor Collins stepped up for announcements, Rick's gaze drifted across the sanctuary.

Lucy sat across the aisle, her hair neatly pulled back, her dress soft and flattering, but she looked pale and washed out beneath the sanctuary lights. Her eyes were swollen, rimmed with exhaustion and Rick gasped as he looked to Lucy's left to catch a glimpse of Eddie who was sitting beside her solemn. His face bore traces of frustration as he watched Collins read the announcements with great reverence and Rick just shook his head in amusement as he settled back into his seat and glanced at the bulletin.

After the final hymn, Rick stood and saw Lucy and Eddie rise from their pew. Lucy was stalled by someone greeting her from the opposite aisle. Eddie, however, stepped into the narrow space between the pews, clearly intending to slip past the crowd.

Rick decided it was the perfect moment for a private word and stepped into the aisle, only to see Elinor reach Eddie first. She was saying something Rick could not hear, her shoulders stiff, her posture tight, her hands animated. There was something fraught in the way she spoke as though she were making a plea rather than making a simple Sunday morning greeting.

Eddie answered, his voice too low to carry, but whatever he said caused Elinor's expression to shutter. She turned away abruptly and for a brief second their eyes caught and Rick saw anger and frustration well up in her eyes before she turned away again. Eddie reached out, as if to stop her, and Rick could not quite tell what might have happened next if Sam had not spotted him at that moment.

"Hey, Uncle Eddie! Aunt Elinor!" Sam shouted, waving enthusiastically across the lawn as he held hands with his Sunday school teacher, Robert Martin.

Startled, Eddie turned away from Elinor. His smile came too fast, too wide. Rick thought that he looked thinner and tired in a way sleep did not fix.

"Hey," Eddie said. "I didn't expect— How are you guys doing?"

"Mr. Martin says you're a hero!" Sam grinned up at Eddie as Rick caught up with them.

"A hero, aye?"

"Yep! I told Sam and our Sunday school class how you gave me that great advice about not hiding behind cowardice and silence." Slapping Eddie enthusiastically on the back, Robert smiled all around. "And, praise God, Harri has forgiven me, Pastor Eddie, and she's even agreed to go to the Valentine's Day dance with me."

"Congratulations, Robert." Eddie smiled tightly at the younger man, who waved and rushed off to find Harri. "Ah, how easy the young people have it."

Rick nodded and glanced toward where Elinor and Marianne were deep in conversation. Noticing the way Eddie kept glancing back at the women as well, Rick decided enough was enough.

"We won't take no for an answer, Eddie. The kids and I miss you, and we want you and Lucy to join us for lunch. Ned and Fanny have already agreed to come. Ned has even threatened to stick me with the check if you don't show."

Eddie hesitated. "Will… will Elinor be—?"

Rick lifted an eyebrow, and they both looked back to where Marianne now stood alone, watching her sister walk toward the parking lot by herself.

With a sigh, Rick turned back to Eddie. "Don't think about it. Like I said—we won't take no."

Eddie sagged dramatically and winked at Sam. "Okay. I know when I'm beaten."

The mood shifted when Lucy and Marianne approached with the rest of the Wentworth kids. Ellie cheered and wrapped her arms around Lucy's waist when Sam said, "You're coming to lunch with us, Aunt Lucy!"

They ended up at Rick's favorite hole-in-the-wall Mexican place, with long tables covered in plastic tablecloths and the air thick with the scent of grilled onions and cilantro. Rick grabbed bottled sodas from the fridge, helped Ellie choose the perfect blue crayon, and guided everyone toward the back patio.

Marianne and Fanny closed ranks around Lucy, drawing her into easy conversation. Rick noticed Eddie hover at the edge, hands in his pockets, eyes tracking Lucy as if afraid she might vanish if he looked away too long.

Chips and salsa arrived at the table.

Oblivious to the tension, Sam asked, "Are you having a boy?"

Rick nudged him, but the damage was already done.

Eddie froze, then smiled—slow and genuine. "We don't know yet."

"A girl!" Ellie declared.

"Miss Marianne delivered a baby in an ambulance last night," Lily announced proudly.

"I did indeed," Marianne said, laughing. "The sweetest little baby boy."

Lucy laughed softly, one hand drifting to her belly. "That is comforting. Never know when we might need help."

Fanny tilted her head, her eyes full of curiosity as she looked at Marianne. "Are your ovaries crying for one of your own?"

Marianne blushed and the adults laughed. The kids stared.

"What ovaries?" Walter demanded.

The subject mercifully shifted.

As lunch wound down and Ned herded the kids toward the arcade with a fistful of quarters, Sam's attention locked onto the open patch of grass beside the restaurant.

"Dad," he said quietly, like this was strategy. "Do you still have the soccer ball in the car?"

Rick winked. "Why do you ask questions you already know the answer to?"

"Because hope is important," Sam said solemnly.

Walter appeared at his side. "If you're playing, I'm playing."

Looking down at her sparkling sandals and pleated skirt, Maggie stepped closer to Lily, folding her arms with mock seriousness. "Then Lily and I will be the commentators."

"We'll give the play-by-play," Lily added firmly. "Because this is very important."

Ellie lifted Quackers like a banner. "We are the rah-rah."

Rick glanced back toward the table. Marianne, Lucy, and Fanny stood together in conversation and didn't look like they'd be going anywhere anytime soon. Eddie, meanwhile, stood several feet away hovering and looking as if he was debating the ethics of disappearing.

Rick hesitated, then Sam did what Sam always did when adults stalled and decided for the group.

"Uncle Eddie!" he called. "Don't you want to play soccer with us?"

The invitation hung between them as Eddie blinked.

"Me?"

"Yes," Sam said. "Two on two. Dad says it builds character."

"I did not say that," Rick muttered.

"He definitely did," Maggie stage-whispered to Lily.

"I heard him," Lily agreed.

Walter assessed Eddie like a coach. "You're tall. You'd be good on defense."

Eddie hesitated slightly and then shrugged with an exhale. "Why not? But, be warned, I'm very rusty."

"That's fine," Sam said generously. "Dad is ancient."

"Hey!"

Ned appeared behind them, coffee in hand. "What's this?"

"We need a referee," Lily declared.

Ned grinned. "I accept this sacred calling."

Teams formed quickly.

"Dad, you're with me," Sam said.

Walter pointed to Eddie. "You're with me."

Rick tossed the ball between his hands. "First goal wins."

"No boo-boos," Ellie warned gravely. "Quackers says."

"I agree with Quackers," Eddie replied solemnly.

Maggie cleared her throat. "And we will be calling fouls."

"Mostly on Dad," Lily added.

Ned blew an imaginary whistle. "Play."

The ball rolled and Sam surged forward with all the confidence of a boy who dreamed of goals. Rick intercepted clumsily, nudging it back. Sam nearly tripped over his own feet, laughing.

"Strong opening drive," Maggie announced.

"Very emotional, Miss Dashwood. Do you think the Ferrars and Wentworth team has a chance of winning?" Lily said.

Walter pivoted sharply, stealing the ball. "We heard that!"

Growling, Sam shouted, "Steal it, Dad!"

Eddie froze, then kicked. The ball sailed wide, smacking the fence.

Maggie winced. "Unfortunate angle for Pastor Eddie. He'll be regretting that when he goes to sleep."

"But excellent effort," Lily said kindly.

Ellie clapped anyway. "Woot woot!"

Ned suggested a reset and Rick passed to Sam, who attempted a move he had clearly practiced on his bed a thousand times. Unfortunately, his foot slipped and the ball rolled free.

"That was a brave move, Sam," Lily declared.

"But poor execution," Maggie added.

"Defense, Uncle Eddie!" Walter yelled.

"I'm defending," Eddie protested, jogging back.

"You're jogging too slow."

"I am doing my best," Eddie said—grinning so wide Rick almost believed his friend was back.

"No arguing with teammates," Ned called.

Rick faked left and passed to Sam. Sam kicked and the ball slid neatly between Eddie's feet.

"Goal!" Lily shouted. "Team Dad-Sam wins!"

Maggie lifted her hands. "Upset victory."

Sam whooped. "Did you see that?"

"I did," Rick said, ruffling his hair.

But what stayed with him was Eddie's grin. It was unguarded and real in a way Rick had not seen in weeks.

Continuing to pan over the group, Rick looked at his children and Maggie. They were all grass-stained, and loud and happy as they decided now was a perfect time to roll around in the grass. His heart swelled with the kind of gratitude that pressed firmly against his ribs.

He knew better, however, than to trust a single good moment to mean the danger had passed.

CHAPTER TWELVE

Some silences don't arrive all at once. Some are built layer by layer, until even breathing feels careful, as if you're afraid of disturbing something fragile.

Eddie unlocked the front door and held it open for Lucy. She stepped inside without looking at him, the lightness of the afternoon falling away the moment the door closed behind them. Her hand brushed her stomach, a habitual motion now, and he looked elsewhere, as though noticing it would require him to say something he was not ready to speak aloud. The house felt too clean, too still, the kind of quiet that settles after laughter has nowhere left to go.

Lucy set her purse on the entryway table and released a slow, nearly soundless breath.

"Lunch was… nice," Eddie suggested. He'd especially loved the ridiculous soccer game in the strip of grass beside the restaurant.

Eddie waited for Lucy to say something. When nothing came, he closed the door with exaggerated care, the click of the latch sounding louder than it should have.

He swallowed. "Rick's kids sure are full of life."

Lucy slipped off her flats and crossed into the kitchen. Eddie followed at a respectful distance, the way a man approaches something already cracked, afraid of breaking it further.

She picked up a pile of circulars and ads, staring without purpose, before dumping them in the recycle bin under the sink. Appearing to struggle to find something to do, she snatched up a mug off the dish rack and rinsed it twice more as Eddie leaned against the counter, then straightened again, as if posture might count for something.

"Marianne invited me to her bachelorette get-together."

He had turned away. He stopped and looked back, his attention entirely on trying to read her body language. "She did?"

She hesitated, fingers worrying her wedding band. She still wore it. That alone felt like mercy he hadn't earned.

"She's having it next weekend," Lucy continued. "It's going to be a small gathering. Tea with the girls, now that Caroline is back from their honeymoon."

"Oh." His throat tightened. "That sounds… nice."

"It does." She shifted her weight. "Except…" Her gaze flicked to the counter. "Elinor will be there."

The name settled between them, heavy and unmoving.

Eddie stayed where he was. "She was at church."

Lucy nodded. "I know. She was sitting with Marianne."

He exhaled slowly. "She came up to me after."

Lucy didn't react. She simply waited.

"It wasn't a long conversation," he said. "Just a few words."

She studied his face, then looked away. "Marianne mentioned Elinor might take Maggie back home to close up the house for a few days later this week." She pressed her fingers to her forehead. "She was trying to be kind. I didn't know what to say."

"You felt trapped."

Her eyes shimmered, exhaustion and hurt pooling together. "You're right. I don't want to say yes. If I'm being honest, I'd rather never see her again. But I didn't know how to say no either. Marianne is one of my best friends."

"You don't have to go," he said, then stopped himself. "I mean—only if you don't want to."

Lucy studied him for a long beat. Eddie tightened his jaw, already wishing he could take the words back.

"You think me avoiding Elinor fixes anything?" An edge crept into her usually gentle voice.

"No." He shook his head. "I don't think that at all. I just… don't want you hurt."

Her shoulders lifted and fell. "I'm already hurt. And we both know whose fault that is."

He closed his eyes briefly. The truth still drew blood.

"But," she continued, "I also don't want to hide. That's not who I am."

"I know." He took a tentative step closer. "Lucy—"

She stepped back.

The recoil landed like a slap—visceral, immediate, devastating. The space between them widened by inches, then by something larger he could not measure.

"Do you want me to talk to Elinor?" The question came out carefully, almost afraid of itself.

Lucy shook her head. "No. I don't want you doing something because you think I want it. I want you to act because it's right."

Eddie nodded slowly. "I can't undo what I broke," he said hoarsely. "But I can stop adding to it."

Lucy moved to the table and sat. She didn't invite him to join her. She didn't forbid it either. After a moment, he took the chair across from her, his hands clasped tightly in front of him. He loosened them. Then clasped them again, unsure where they belonged now.

A thin strip of afternoon sun stretched across the table, stopping just short of her fingertips—as if even the light wasn't sure how close it was allowed to get.

"I don't hate her," Lucy murmured. "That's the strange part. I don't want her near us. But she isn't the villain. She's just... still living inside an old story she hasn't let go of yet."

Eddie swallowed. "I should have shut that story down years ago."

"You should have shut it down in December," she corrected. "When she came back to town."

His ribs felt too small to contain the ache.

"I know," he said. "You're right."

Lucy looked down at her hands. "I just wish you'd stood up for us."

There was no defense left. No explanation that didn't sound like cowardice dressed up as compassion.

"I'm sorry," he said quietly. "I am so sorry."

For a moment, she let her gaze rest on him. He could see the effort it took—the choice to lean toward forgiveness, toward love—because that was who she was.

"I know," she whispered. "I know you are."

The silence that followed felt different. Less hostile. More fragile.

He did not deserve this woman, or the life she had uprooted so he could follow his calling, or the patience she kept offering when he had given her so little certainty in return.

Lucy stood first, smoothing her sweater. "I'm going to take a nap before youth choir rehearsal." Her eyes flicked briefly toward the hall.

"I'd like—" He stopped, drew a breath. "Yes. I'd like that."

She nodded and walked away.

Eddie remained seated, pressing his palms to his eyes.

He had been praying for a lightning bolt—a miracle big enough to erase the fracture.

But maybe miracles did not always begin with lightning. Maybe they began with staying. With a wife who had not given up yet, and a God who refused to let him rot in self-pity.

After a moment, Eddie stood and followed her down the hall—not to fix anything, not to speak, but simply to stay. One small step at a time.

CHAPTER THIRTEEN

Maggie's laughter carried across the driveway before Rick even
stepped onto the porch.

Elinor tugged a suitcase from the backseat while Marianne juggled
a duffel bag and a crooked stack of books. Maggie waved wildly the
moment she spotted him.

"Hey, Rick! I'm here! Really here!"

"Looks like it." He grinned. "Planning to stay longer than a week
this time?"

"Forever!"

The mind boggled. Rick smiled down at her as she threw her arms
around his middle and raced off to the front door. To think that
this young girl was young enough to be his daughter and yet in fact
going to be his sister-in-law in a matter of weeks.

The front door burst open.

"MAGGIE!"

Lily barreled down the steps with Walter and Sam close behind. Ellie toddled after them tugging Quackers upside down in one arm and her stuffed penguin, Flippers, in her other hand.

Maggie barely dropped her backpack before Lily collided with her in a hug.

"You're really moving here?"

"For real! We're going to be a real family in just a few weeks!"

"You can sleep in my room!" Lily announced. "Daddy said we can pull the trundle back out. Or if you want, you can have my bed and I'll sleep on the floor. I can sleep anywhere after living in the basement."

"Okay, breathe." Rick lifted both hands in mock defeat. "No one is going to be sleeping on the floor or in the basement."

Elinor laughed softly, brushing hair from Maggie's face. "We appreciate the enthusiasm."

Maggie crouched to Ellie's level. "Hey there, Quackers and Flippers."

Ellie nodded solemnly. "They say hi, too."

"We'll show you the beach," Walter added.

"And the arcade," Sam piled on.

"We already have, you sillies!" Lily teased as she grabbed Maggie's hand.

"Daniel's excited too," Ellie declared, just as the puppy trotted out and licked Maggie's hand.

Maggie laughed again, bright and unguarded. "This is the coolest thing ever. We're going to have so much fun."

Rick's kids dragged her inside, each competing for attention, Daniel scrambling along behind them.

Rick caught Marianne's hand once the coast was clear and kissed her fingers. "We're really doing this?" he murmured, half-laughing. Maggie moving in made everything feel permanent.

Marianne smiled, but her eyes flicked briefly to Elinor who was watchful, already reverting to her standoffishness.

Elinor locked the car, exhaling. "They're quite a welcoming committee."

"They mean well."

Marianne stepped closer, slipping an arm through Elinor's. "You don't have to carry everything in tonight. We can sort Maggie's bags out later."

Elinor gave a small, grateful nod. "Thank you."

Maggie reappeared in the doorway, bouncing on her heels. "Hey, you slow pokes! Aren't you guys going to come inside? We're hungry. Can we order some pizzas or are you cooking something, Marianne? I vote for pizza and Lily wants to get hamburgers."

"Pizza," Sam called from behind Maggie. "With breadsticks!"

"Breadsticks and pizza together?" Marianne asked with a twinkle in her eye.

"And hamburgers!" Lily could be heard shouting from inside the house.

With a laugh, Rick shrugged and stood back as he watched Marianne herd Maggie and the kids back toward the house. She paused just long enough to meet Rick's eyes. There was a question left unspoken.

Rick nodded once and turned to help Elinor with the bags.

Elinor shifted the strap of her bag on her shoulder. "You holding up?" Rick asked quietly.

"I'm trying. It's been a lot with finalizing the move. Maggie's excited and Marianne, of course, is ecstatic." She hesitated. "It's the right decision. Everything is just happening so fast."

He took the heavier duffel from the trunk. "You're with family here."

They walked toward the porch together and could hear the sounds of laughter, running feet, and Daniel barking coming from inside.

Rick knew then that if he didn't speak now, he never would. He had seen enough—at church, in the urgency of her words to Eddie, in the way she had turned away when Rick caught her eye. Whatever was between his future sister-in-law and good friend was not finished and he would be failing her, and everyone else, if he didn't say something.

At the door, Rick stopped. Elinor did too.

"So," he said evenly, "do you have a boyfriend?"

He caught Marianne's look of caution as she paused at the door before retreating to the kitchen.

Elinor's chin lifted a fraction. "No."

"Then you need to know this." His voice stayed calm. "Lucy's pregnant."

Shock crossed her face—raw and unguarded. Then something sharper followed.

"I didn't know."

"I figured. But now you do."

"Hey guys," Marianne interrupted gently, "I'm going to pick up the pizzas."

Elinor and Rick both nodded and watched as she rushed to her car, purse slung over her shoulder.

As soon as they were alone on the porch again, Elinor folded her arms and turned to face him. "Rick, whatever you think happened—"

"I know what I saw Sunday," he said, firm but not loud. "You kissed a married man. No, not on Sunday but on New Year's Eve. Honestly? I don't care who initiated the kiss and who ended it. All I know is that you had a choice at Darcy's wedding and you have another choice now. I hope you will choose wisely, because there are a lot of lives that can be hurt by what happens next."

"I've loved Eddie since freshman year," Elinor said quietly. "My feelings cannot just disappear because they are inconvenient."

With a sigh, Rick wondered if this conversation could go anywhere useful.

"Elinor," he tried more softly, "you are my family now. I'm not here to judge you or be cruel to you. But Eddie and Lucy are in a very vulnerable place right now and with the baby they're expecting we need to support and help them. Whatever was going on with you and Eddie on Sunday isn't helping things. Can you understand that?"

Her throat worked. "I never wanted to hurt him…or Lucy."

"But you did. There's no sugarcoating it. Intent does not erase impact."

Her eyes flashed. "I'm not the villain in this drama you've imagined! I did not set out to break a marriage. You seem to forget that I was with Eddie first long before he ever met Lucy Steele. Sometimes God brings people back for a reason. What if He brought you and your college ex back together? Wouldn't you run and take that chance?"

"Are you asking me to if I would choose to take Annie back over your sister?" Rick held her gaze until she dropped her eyes. "Elinor, sometimes God brings people back into our lives to show us what we still haven't surrendered to Him."

The silence stretched until it was almost suffocating.

"Lucy knows you'll be at the bachelorette party," he added. "Marianne didn't want her blindsided."

Elinor closed her eyes, breathing steadily. "Right."

"And now that you know about the baby," Rick said, "I'm just asking you not to make this any harder than it needs to be."

Her jaw tightened, but her voice stayed level. "I hear you."

Marianne returned then, setting a stack of pizzas with deliberate normalcy. "Dinner is here."

"No burgers and breadsticks?" Elinor tried to make a joke of it.

Marianne smirked and shook her head as she stepped inside the house. Rick could hear the room erupt with laughter, running feet and the joys of life continuing, whether they were ready or not.

"MAGGIE, COME SEE THE FORT!"

"And the pantry!"

"And the backyard!"

"Daniel went potty!"

Elinor exhaled. "I don't know who needs more supervision—your kids or my sister."

"Depends on the day." Rick smiled. "We good, Elinor?"

Giving him a long look, Elinor nodded and patted his shoulder.

"Good. And for the record, you can rest assured that I have firmly closed all dreams and hopes about Annie and your sister is my number one priority, aside from the children."

He couldn't read the expression in Elinor's eyes before her expression went neutral but the nod was all he needed as they walked inside.

Later, after the house settled and Elinor left, Rick led Marianne onto the porch, hoping for peace and quiet. When he leaned in to kiss her nose, he stopped short at her expression.

"What did I do?"

She touched his cheek before sitting. "Elinor is my sister. I know what she did. I'm not excusing it. But she's hurting. And you confronting her like that—it felt like choosing sides."

"I am choosing sides," Rick said evenly. "I'm choosing the marriage that exists over the fantasy she's holding."

"She's not a bad person."

"I didn't say she was."

"Then don't treat her like one."

Rick breathed slowly. "I'm trying to stop more damage."

She didn't answer.

"If our roles were reversed," he asked quietly, "what would you want me to do?"

Her eyes met his.

"What if Annie showed up tomorrow?" he continued. "Newly single and said God brought her back because we needed a second chance. What if she kissed me?"

Marianne froze.

"You know what she meant to me. The what-ifs." He let it sit. "How would that feel?"

Her chin trembled. "It would break me."

"I know." He took her hand. "Same if Greg showed up chasing you. I wouldn't allow it—not for a second. That's the situation Eddie and Lucy are in right now."

A shaky breath left her.

"I wasn't attacking Elinor," Rick explained gently. "I was asking her to see the truth."

Marianne covered her face, then lowered her hands. "I don't want to fight."

"Neither do I."

She leaned into him. "I'm scared. Of hurting her. Of losing her. Of being caught in between."

"You're loving her by telling the truth."

"She won't see it that way."

"Not yet."

"I don't want her to ruin our wedding."

"She won't," Rick said firmly. "I won't let her."

"And you're not angry with me?"

He met her eyes. "You're the woman I'm marrying. I couldn't be angry with you if I tried."

Her smile wavered, then held.

"Okay."

She rested against his chest as the porch lights hummed softly around them.

They weren't choosing comfort. They were choosing marriage— and the hard mercy that came with it.

Chapter Fourteen

The house felt wrong in its stillness. Eddie recognized it immediately—not the quiet that came with peace, but the kind that lingered after words had been left unsaid. It was the quiet of restraint, of someone choosing silence over honesty, and he knew he was the reason for it.

He closed the front door gently and set his keys in the ceramic bowl by the entryway. The clink of metal against clay sounded far too loud, as if the house itself were keeping score.

"You're home early."

Lucy's voice drifted from the kitchen—calm, but held together with a practiced steadiness he recognized too well. It was the same tone she used at doctor's appointments and church functions. The tone of someone determined not to ask the wrong question.

"I rearranged some things."

He didn't add the truth—that he couldn't sit in the coffee shop all day pretending to read theology while feeling like an intruder in his own life. He hadn't even turned a page.

He drew a breath and stepped into the kitchen.

Lucy stood at the counter chopping vegetables, her movements careful, measured, as if precision might keep everything from coming apart. She wore the striped tunic and dark blue leggings she'd reached for nearly every day that week. He noticed the way her shoulders stayed tight, the way she shifted her weight as if standing too long already cost her something.

She didn't look up at first, and he braced for silence—but then she spoke.

"How was your afternoon?"

"Fine."

Her knife paused mid-slice. Not dramatically—just long enough to register.

"Fine?" she echoed.

He cleared his throat. "Just… ordinary."

She nodded once. "Ordinary sounds good."

The words landed heavy. Ordinary used to be easy for them. Ordinary had once meant shared jokes, easy evenings, prayer before bed. Now it felt like something they were pretending to remember how to do, like a language neither of them spoke fluently anymore.

He reached for a glass, grateful for something to do with his hands. "Do you want water?"

"No, thank you."

He hated how polite she was being. Silence hummed between them—thin, stretched, ready to snap if either of them leaned too hard.

"How are you feeling?" His voice stayed low, careful.

Her eyes lifted briefly. The exhaustion there was unmistakable, worn deep beneath the surface. She pressed her lips together before answering, as if choosing words that would hurt the least.

"The baby is fine," she said quietly. "I'm just tired."

The answer carried more than he wanted to hear. It always did.

"You should sit down."

"I will. After dinner prep."

He nodded, then shifted too quickly, reaching for safer ground. "Did you hear back about the double date that Fanny wanted to plan?"

Her shoulders stilled. The knife resumed its rhythm, slower now.

"Yes. Fanny texted and said they're free anytime."

He waited, hoping she might say more. She didn't.

"I think we should wait until after Rick and Marianne's engagement party."

Her tone stayed gentle, but the meaning was clear.

I can't pretend in front of people yet. I can barely pretend here.

He swallowed. "That makes sense."

She released a breath that trembled despite her effort to steady it. "I can't say I'm looking forward to the party. I had enough of being in the same group as Elinor at Marianne's bachelorette this weekend."

His stomach sank.

Lucy had gone because she loved Marianne. Because she was loyal. Because she didn't want to be the person who made things awkward.

"That makes sense," he murmured again, uselessly, hating how easily the words came when they required nothing of him.

Shame tightened his chest as he walked down the hall to his office. He told himself he needed the quiet. He told himself distance was wisdom. He told himself he would come back in a minute.

The door clicked shut behind him.

He didn't know how to fix what he'd helped break. When Robert Martin had asked him for similar advice, he'd hesitated—but at least he had known what to say. He had spoken clearly, firmly, about repentance and repair. About telling the truth and telling one of the girls that there was no hope.

Why couldn't he rescue his own marriage just as easily?

The air in his home office felt heavier than the rest of the house. His sermon notebook lay open on the desk where he'd abandoned it weeks ago, the pages curling slightly at the edges. Ever since Rick had gently asked if he'd considered preaching again, Eddie had circled the question like a man afraid to touch something sacred.

He didn't know if he would ever feel worthy of the pulpit again— or if stepping back had become another way to hide.

He stared at a half-finished outline from the first week after New Year's, back when everything cracked apart. The passage was underlined twice. Words about confession. Restoration. Light.

None of them felt like they belonged to him anymore.

His phone vibrated and he sent it straight to voicemail. He almost ignored it until the transcript preview flashed across the screen.

Elinor came by the church office… upset… asking for you…

His pulse stumbled.

After making sure the door was securely shut, he pressed play.

"Pastor Eddie? Hi, it's Mrs. Morland. I know you're on sabbatical, but I thought you should know Elinor Dashwood stopped by today. She was very distressed and insisted she needed to speak with you. We told her you weren't available, but she wouldn't leave a message. I just… I didn't feel right not letting you know."

The message ended. Stillness thickened around him.

Elinor had come looking for him.

Had this been before or after the bachelorette party Lucy had mentioned?

A cold memory flickered—New Year's Eve, the patio at Rick's house, her bright eyes looking up at him as if he hung the stars and the moon, and the kiss he should have stopped faster. Everything had shifted in that moment without his consent, and yet somehow entirely because of it.

Tugging his sweater off, Eddie sighed as he tossed it into a ball in the corner. Lucy had sensed something at the bachelorette party. Now he knew she was right.

He didn't call Elinor back and he didn't return to the kitchen.

Instead, he sat while the sun crept slowly across the carpet, and the house settled into a quiet that felt less like peace and more like waiting. It was undoubtedly waiting for him to decide whether he would act, or continue letting time decide for him. And the problem was he wasn't even sure himself what road he was taking.

A soft knock tapped the door.

"Dinner's ready."

"I'll be there in a minute."

Lucy lingered on the other side of the door. Eddie could hear her measured and careful breathing on the other side. After a moment, her steps moved away.

And yet, he still didn't move.

His gaze drifted back to the sermon notebook. He picked up a pen, his hand trembling, and crossed out the old outline with a single, decisive line before writing:

Truth always costs something.
Running won't stop the debt from coming due.

Eddie stared at the words until they blurred. He didn't know when he would pay. He only knew that the account was no longer quiet.

And it would come due soon.

Chapter Fifteen

Sometimes, maybe more often than we admit, love looks like showing up with pizza and refusing to let a man sit alone in the dark.

If joy had a sound tonight, it was bowling pins collapsing beneath Sam's triumphant victory scream.

"STRIKE!"

Sam launched into a victory dance that involved raised fists, an off-key shout, and nearly tripping over the return rack. Walter whooped. George Knightley lifted one hand in a restrained but genuine clap, his cane propped neatly beside his chair, already entering the score with the careful concentration of a man who liked numbers to behave.

Darcy lowered his arm like a superhero who had just saved a nation—perfectly on brand for a man who had honeymooned in Paris and returned insufferably serene.

"Still showing off," Rick called.

Darcy smirked. "Some men bring home Eiffel Tower keychains. I bring home superior athletic form."

Walter groaned. "How does Aunt Caroline put up with you?"

Rick leaned back in his seat and took in the scene before him. Darcy had brought them bowling for Rick's first birthday outing in ten years. The last time they had come, Rick had barely been out of the hospital and still used a cane. Darcy graciously enough rented a special assistance ramp so Rick wouldn't have to bear the full weight.

Now Rick was on his own two feet, keeping up with his children and his friends.

After assuring the boys that Aunt Caroline loved this enthusiastic and happy version of himself, Darcy dropped into the molded plastic seat beside Rick, the chair creaking under his long frame. He studied Rick's face the way only someone who'd known him since kindergarten could—without rushing, without flinching.

"You look good," Darcy said quietly.

Rick snorted. "I don't recall paying you to butter me up tonight."

"The boys think you need cheering," Darcy murmured. "Should I be concerned?"

"They're too perceptive for their own good."

Darcy didn't answer right away. He just watched him with that unsettling blend of affection and precision. Rick felt the unspoken question hovering there.

Then, as if deciding not to push yet, Darcy stood and grabbed his ball.

To the boys' cheers, Darcy bowled another strike.

Rick shook his head as Darcy returned. "Was your honeymoon really that amazing?"

Darcy's expression softened completely. "Yes. Better than I expected. I still can't believe I waited this long to put my ring on Caroline's finger."

Rick smiled, but he looked away before envy could take root.

It wasn't a European honeymoon he wanted. He would have been perfectly content with a quiet week at the beach cottage, as long as Marianne was beside him. And yet the fears that had started to claw at him since proposing to Marianne hadn't entirely loosened their grip.

Some days, he still wondered if Marianne deserved someone steadier and less aware of how fragile joy could be.

"Dad!" Sam sprinted over, breathless. "It's your turn!"

"And you have to beat Uncle Darcy," Walter added. "Because he won't shut up otherwise."

Rick laughed, stood, and accepted the ball with exaggerated solemnity. He took a moment longer than necessary, feeling the familiar weight in his hand. The polished lane gleamed back at him, reflecting more than he wanted to see—past versions of himself, injured and afraid.

He bowled.

The ball curved clean and true, catching the sweet spot. All ten pins fell in a dramatic, satisfying collapse.

Sam roared. Walter applauded. George entered the score with reverent approval as Darcy sighed with an exaggerated groan.

Rick returned to his seat with a theatrical bow and raised his eyebrow at his best friend. Darcy narrowed his eyes. "I don't like this development."

"So," Darcy said a moment later, casual but not careless, "you and Marianne confirmed for the Bertrams' retreat?"

Rick nodded. "She already has a color-coded packing list. She says it's going to be the absolute—emphasis on the word *absolute*—best honeymoon ever."

Darcy didn't smile this time. Something steadier settled into his expression.

"Rick… I want to give that to you."

Rick blinked. "Give what to me?"

"Your honeymoon," Darcy said. "A week or two in London before the retreat. Flights, a hotel, and whatever flowers Marianne likes. I'd like to pay for it as my wedding gift."

Rick stared, then shook his head hard enough to risk whiplash. "No. Absolutely not. Darcy, I can't even afford to dream about London. I still owe the kids' dentist for cavity fillings. And I can never repay you for everything you've already done. Bath already feels unreal."

Darcy let him finish. Then he said gently, "You're not paying."

"That's a ridiculous expense."

"You pay me back every time I look at you and see you safe," Darcy replied. "Knowing you're alive and no longer trapped in what Louisa did to you is payment enough. Let me give you this. You know I have the money."

Rick swallowed and looked away, blinking harder than he wanted to.

Darcy lowered his voice. "Caroline told me Marianne mentioned how much she loved the idea of England. I want that for you."

It wasn't guilt Darcy offered. It was love—and that made the gift nearly impossible to refuse.

"I'll think about it," Rick said.

Darcy smiled like a lawyer who already knew he'd won.

Later, after pizza boxes were stacked and two exhausted boys slumped half-asleep in their seats, Rick stepped aside to return the bowling shoes. Darcy joined him at the counter.

"On a different note," Darcy murmured, "I expected to see Eddie tonight."

Rick's chest tightened. "I don't know what's going on," he said carefully. "But something is."

Darcy studied him. "Has he said anything?"

Rick shook his head. "He keeps talking about *waiting*. About needing clarity. About letting things unfold in God's time."

Darcy's mouth thinned. "That sounds familiar."

Rick nodded. He knew the language too well. He had used it himself not too long ago.

"The retreat might force something," Darcy said quietly.

Rick thought of the retreat.

If Eddie didn't come—

If he did—

Either way, something was about to break.

"Hurry!" Sam shouted, already in his socks. "We're getting ice cream!"

"Where did this burst of energy come from?" Rick laughed, but he thanked the attendant and followed the boys out anyway.

On the drive home, the coastal air swept through the open windows ushering in the salty breeze Rick could never get enough of.

His thoughts churned. His best friend Darcy was offering him a honeymoon. Eddie was disappearing into carefully chosen spiritual language. Rick had joy, Darcy was behaving as though he'd won the jackpot of marriages, and Eddie was sinking beneath words that sounded faithful but asked nothing of him.

Proximity is how God protects people, Marianne had said.

Tonight, Rick believed her.

He carried Sam inside to be met warmly by Marianne while Walter trudged behind, clutching the remains of his ice cream cone. The pantry door bore a construction-paper sign in Lily's handwriting:

WELCOME HOME SUPERHEROES
(with a lion wearing a cape)

Rick smiled as he kissed Marianne goodnight and tucked his boys into bed before going to peek in on his daughters.

He really was getting married in a few weeks and Lord willing he would soon have a passport stamp from England. But first, he was going to have to walk straight into the dark with a friend who kept insisting he was waiting on the light.

CHAPTER SIXTEEN

Lucy hummed softly as she braided her hair in the bathroom mirror. It was barely more than a thread of sound, a tune he couldn't place, but it loosened something Eddie hadn't even realized he'd been holding in.

She was wearing a cobalt blue wrap dress that happened to be one of Eddie's favorite dresses. The pregnancy had enhanced her curves, and though Eddie knew she felt self-conscious, he thought she had never been more beautiful.

"You're staring," she murmured, catching his expression in the glass.

He had been careful not to look too closely since the test. The pregnancy had become something to manage rather than something to *feel.* Yet, as he stepped behind her, the familiar scent of her perfume tugged something at his heart. "You look beautiful."

Her cheeks warmed. "Thank you."

He lifted his hand and rested it gently over her belly. She stilled beneath his touch. In the mirror, her eyes met his with a mix of hope and caution in a way that frightened him more than anger ever could.

"Do you think," she asked quietly, "we can make it work?"

He tightened his fingers around waist and buried his face in her hair. The answer rose instinctively, smooth and practiced. "I don't think God brought us this far just to leave us here."

Her lip trembled as she blinked. "We should go. If I cry, Marianne will assume you said something romantic."

"Heaven forbid," he said lightly, grateful for the deflection.

The drive was quiet, but not brittle. Lucy kept her hand on her stomach. Eddie's eyes drifted there again and again, like a prayer he hadn't learned how to say out loud.

After a mile, he asked, "Do you want to go to the couples retreat?"

She glanced at him. "Do you want to?"

"Yes," he said after a beat. "I want help. And we couldn't have better friends to do this with."

She nodded slowly. "You're right. I can't pretend everything is fine, but maybe the retreat can help." She hesitated. "Whatever happens, Eddie, I don't want this baby arriving into the awkward mess we've been calling home."

Her honesty cut clean.

"We'll make sure he or she doesn't," he declared, clinging to certainty.

They turned onto Rick's street. String lights traced the roofline. A banner stretched across the porch rail:

CONGRATS RICK & MARIANNE

Children's handwriting and drawings spilled around the letters. Eddie recognized Lily's careful strokes immediately, and Ellie's penguin drawings were unmistakable.

Lucy smiled softly as he opened her door. "The kids definitely organized that."

"Without question."

Then Eddie froze mid-step.

Elinor's silver sedan was parked halfway up the street, tucked behind Darcy's SUV.

Lucy saw it a heartbeat later. Her hand tightened on her purse.

"Oh."

"Did you plan to see her tonight?" she asked quietly.

"No," he said immediately.

She nodded once. "All right."

But it wasn't enough.

He reached for an explanation. "She is the sister of the bride."

"That's not what I asked," Lucy said gently.

He flinched. She withdrew her hand under the pretense of straightening her dress.

"Do you remember what you told me after New Year's?" she asked. "When I asked if there was anything else I needed to know?"

"I said I'd draw clearer lines," he murmured.

"And what you didn't say," she replied, "was that there were no lines at all."

Before he could answer, the front door opened. Ned and Fanny stepped out mid-laugh and stopped when they saw Lucy's face.

Fanny crossed the distance at once. "Lucy, darling, you look lovely."

Lucy smiled thinly. "Thank you. I feel like a walking secret."

"You won't be able to hide this one much longer," Fanny said gently, her eyes flicking to Lucy's middle and then back up to her pinched expression. "Lucy, I wanted to show you the cross-stitch I started. Would you like to see it? It's in the car."

Lucy nodded. "Of course."

She brushed past Eddie, her sleeve grazing his arm. It was a fleeting contact that felt like a farewell and made Eddie want to grab her back and haul her into the car and drive far, far away.

"I'll be right back," she murmured.

Eddie could only nod as she followed Fanny away, leaving him with Ned.

"Edward," Ned said quietly.

"Pastor."

"Does she still believe there's a chance?" Ned asked, glancing toward Elinor, who was stepping out of the house at that very moment.

Eddie swallowed. "She knows I'm married."

Ned kept his gaze fixed on him. "That's not what I asked."

"Hello, Eddie."

The sound of Elinor's voice tightened something around his throat.

"Um—hello, Elinor," he said, forcing a smile. "You're looking well tonight."

The moment she grinned and glanced down at her floral dress, he knew he had erred and gasped aloud.

"You all right?" Ned murmured. "You look like you've swallowed something bitter."

"I—we forgot Rick and Marianne's gift," Eddie blurted.

Elinor laughed awkwardly and patted his shoulder. "There are so many gifts in there that it won't be missed."

Ned coughed sharply. "Ah. I believe Fanny is signaling us."

Taking Eddie's arm, Ned steered him firmly up the street.

"You do realize my car is in the opposite direction," Eddie muttered.

"Shut up," Ned hissed, stopping abruptly.

For the first time, Eddie saw his friend not as a pastor but as a tired, aging man pulled unwittingly into someone else's mess.

"You keep letting her think there's room," Ned quietly scolded.

"I don't want to hurt her," Eddie whispered.

"We don't heal pain by pretending it isn't there," Ned replied. "You have to close the door, Eddie. Completely."

By the time they reached the Bertrams' car, Lucy was in the process of fastening her seat belt in the back seat. Fanny sat calmly in the front, hands folded in her lap and her expression hidden behind sunglasses.

"Lucy." Eddie stepped closer, his eyes catching on the strap across her chest, and a familiar anxiety tightened in his throat. "We can go in together now if you're feeling better. Elinor's gone, so we don't—"

She shook her head, not looking at him. "I saw you with her."

"I was just trying to be nice. Ned was with me."

"Stop," Lucy said softly. "Nice is one of the most overused words in the world." Her voice trembled. "I don't need nice. I need a husband who chooses me."

She closed her eyes. "I'm tired, Eddie. I'm going to stay with the Bertrams tonight. I need somewhere I can breathe."

Something inside him split.

"Can I come?"

Her expression twisted with love and grief. "I want the man I married. The one who climbed onto a coffee-shop counter and shouted that he loved me."

She inhaled slowly. "Tonight, you need to decide who you're going to be."

"I still love you," she said, meeting his eyes. "But I will not share you."

The door closed.

Pastor Ned squeezed Eddie's shoulder as he walked around to get in the front seat and before he had even realized what happened the car pulled away.

The house behind him glowed with warmth. Laughter drifted through open windows. The banner fluttered above him, but all Eddie could see was the empty space where Lucy had stood.

People left in twos and threes. Eventually, the street quieted. All the while, Eddie remained beneath the streetlamp, unable to deny that standing still had finally becoming more painful than choosing. At last, he drew a breath that scraped his lungs, climbed the steps, and knocked on the door.

CHAPTER SEVENTEEN

Rick's Journal

Joy does not erase memory.

Sometimes it stands beside it, asking you to live anyway.

The house had finally settled into the gentle quiet that followed a long day of celebration. A stray balloon bumped lazily against the hallway wall. The faint scent of orange zest lingered near the dessert table. Rick gathered the last stack of plates and carried them into the kitchen, smiling at the sight of the cannoli cake, or what remained of it.

The kids had insisted on baking it themselves. Caroline had supervised, but Lily had taken the lead, determined it would be just like the cake Rick's mom used to make. She had approached the task with the seriousness of someone entrusted with something sacred.

At times he could almost forget that she was only a nine-year-old child. She was so mature and yet at other times like this morning it'd been abundantly clear that she was as vulnerable if not more so than others. George Knightley had steadied her nerves that morning when she'd panicked thinking she'd ruined the cake and had run across the sand next door. Rick would never forget the way Lily's shoulders had finally relaxed when he found and told her she didn't have to earn his love with anything she did.

The cake had, in fact, been good—better than good—and Lily's proud smile when Marianne cut the first slice had been worth every anxious moment.

Rick set the plates beside the sink and listened to the low murmur of voices from the den, where Marianne was helping the kids rebuild the fort they'd received for Christmas. The joyful sounds filled the house in a way that still felt faintly miraculous, as if they might disappear if Rick named the joy too loudly.

Rick heard the thump of a cane approaching and looked up to see George appear in the doorway with his coat folded over his arm.

"Heading out?" Rick asked.

George nodded. "Your crew insisted I could not leave without a complete tour of the redesign of the fort."

Rick smiled. "Lily narrated, I assume."

"With impressive detail," George said. "The cake was something special. You should be proud."

Rick swallowed. "Thank you, George, for this morning."

George rested a hand briefly on Rick's shoulder. "Anytime."

The latch clicked softly behind him and a moment later, the doorbell rang. Rick opened the door expecting someone to have forgotten a scarf or jacket. Instead, he broke into a grin.

"Eddie?"

Before his friend could speak, Rick pulled him into a huge hug.

"You're here," Rick said. "I was starting to think you were going to miss the fun."

Eddie smiled faintly as he stepped inside. "I didn't want the night to end without stopping by."

Rick heard the weight beneath the words, the careful way they were arranged. He didn't press. Eddie was here. That was what mattered.

Before Rick could say more, Marianne stepped out from the den, brushing a dusting of glitter from her hands. She crossed to Rick easily, slipping beneath his arm as he bent to kiss her forehead.

"Hey, Eddie," she said warmly. "Sorry we missed you earlier."

Eddie straightened at once. "Lucy wanted to come. She just wasn't feeling well."

Marianne's hand settled briefly at his elbow. "First trimester nausea can be rough. Hopefully she turns a corner soon."

"From your lips to God's ears," Eddie said, managing a small smile.

A moment later, he excused himself, murmuring something about the late hour. Rick walked him to the door and watched as Eddie, shoulders slightly hunched, disappeared into the quiet of the night. Rick's chest tightened with worry as he recognized the same polite words and careful smiles he, too, had hidden behind countless times before.

The gate clicked again, pulling Rick out of his thoughts. This time, the new arrivals were accompanied by soft laughter. Darcy and Caroline stepped inside, cheeks flushed from a walk along the waterfront. They carried the easy glow of newlyweds still marveling at the simple miracle of choosing each other.

"You two look like you wandered out of a wedding brochure," Rick groaned as he pulled Marianne closer, slipping his arm around her shoulder.

Caroline laughed. "We got caught talking about Paris again."

"Again?" Marianne teased.

Darcy lifted a brow. "Trying to see if we can slip back over before my next case."

"Being a lawyer must be exhausting," Marianne said dryly, dodging Darcy's playful reach.

Rick cleared his throat. "There's something I haven't told you yet."

Marianne turned to him. "That sounds ominous."

"Do you remember saying the retreat in Bath felt like the perfect honeymoon?"

Her expression softened. "I still think that."

"Well," Rick continued slowly, "Darcy made us an offer."

Marianne blinked. "An offer?"

"Would you want to go to London with me first? As an actual honeymoon?"

She stared at him, breath catching. "London. You and me?"

Darcy grinned. "Rick was hoping to take me, but Caroline insisted it was only right for him to bring his wife."

Marianne laughed, her joy spilling free and causing Rick to laugh too.

Rick squeezed her hand. "Yes, Sunshine. You and me."

Her hand flew to her mouth. "Rick, that's a dream. But what about the kids?"

Caroline stepped forward. "That's all covered. They'll have so much fun they won't want to come home."

Darcy nodded. "George volunteered to handle watching the kids while we're at the retreat and Caroline and I will fill them up on sugar while they're staying with us before that that they won't even know you're gone."

Marianne's eyes filled. "You would really do that? Even Maggie?"

"Gladly," Caroline confirmed as she leaned forward and kissed Marianne's cheek.

"Yes," Marianne said, her joy bubbling out. "Absolutely yes. A thousand times yes, please!"

Rick pulled her close, catching Darcy's satisfied smirk and shook his head in amazement. They were really going to London for a honeymoon.

"Start your list, folks," Caroline said. "Museums. Tea rooms. Bookshops. You have no idea how much there is to see and do. I don't think Darcy and I even covered a tenth of what we'd planned."

Marianne laughed. "I already have one."

Rick kissed her temple. "Of course you do."

After Darcy and Caroline left, Rick followed Marianne onto the porch. Lanterns cast a soft glow across the boards. Beyond the dunes, the waves rolled in a steady rhythm that felt like a long-awaited release.

"It feels good out here," Rick said unnecessarily as Marianne leaned into him. "It feels like we can finally exhale."

The screen door creaked.

"Couldn't sleep, Sweetheart?" Rick asked.

Lily stood there in her pajamas, Leo her stuffed animal tucked under one arm. Her eyes were heavy but peaceful.

"I just wanted to say goodnight," she whispered.

Marianne shifted to make space. Lily climbed between them, warm and trusting, and Rick wrapped an arm around her as the swing began to move.

"The sky looks happy tonight," Lily murmured.

Rick smiled. "It should. You worked hard today."

"You know what's coming up soon?" Marianne asked.

"Our wedding?" Lily guessed.

"That too," Marianne said. "But your tenth birthday."

Rick's throat tightened. *Ten.* Something that was remarkable for most children because of the double digits was miraculous in Rick's mind. His little girl was going to experience her first birthday outside of the basement and surrounded by all three of her siblings.

Lily settled more fully against him, sleep overtaking her. Rick rested his cheek against her hair, memory pressing close—of cold nights, whispered prayers, and the terror of almost losing her last year.

Now she was here and safe in his arms.

"Goodnight, Sweetheart," he whispered.

The swing drifted slowly. Lantern light swayed with it. Marianne's hand rested over his heart, steady and sure.

Rick let himself sit fully in the truth of the moment. His daughter was safe. His family was whole. His future no longer felt like something he had to outrun.

London waited for Marianne and him. The retreat waited for them and their friends. And for the first time in a very long while, Rick was not afraid of what came next.

Part II

Rick's Journal

Love taught me how to stand again. Now it's teaching me how to stand for the people I'd walk through fire for.

CHAPTER EIGHTEEN

Eddie cut the ignition and rested his forehead against the steering wheel, his breath fogging up the window. Lucy had returned from the Bertrams' today. He had told himself all afternoon that he was ready to see her. Now that the time was here, fear pressed in from every side.

After a long moment, he reached for the bouquet of daisies he had chosen at the florist and forced himself out of the car.

The house was quiet when he stepped inside and the silence unsettled him. For a moment, he wondered if Lucy had changed her mind again and gone back to Ned and Fanny.

He shed his coat and moved down the hallway, each step heavier than the last. Everything looked exactly as he had left it earlier. Everything, that is, until he reached the bedrooms. Their door stood cracked open.

Lucy lay curled on her side, one hand tucked beneath her cheek, the blanket resting low on her shoulder. The soft curls in her hair made something loosen in his chest. She looked as though she had tried to be lovely for him. Then his gaze dropped. He saw the gentle curve of her belly—small but unmistakable.

It was hard to believe that their child was growing in her stomach.

Showing up, he realized, was only the beginning. He had known
that for weeks, but standing there in the doorway, something inside
him went still, as if it had finally understood what was at stake.

He set the flowers on his side of the bed and crossed quietly to the
old armchair next to Lucy's side of the bed. Lowering himself into
the seat, he leaned forward, elbows braced on his knees. Lucy slept
on, unaware of him.

"You are carrying our child," he whispered. "And I am the one
who made you doubt you were loved. How could you ever forgive
me?"

He stayed there through the night, keeping watch like a man too
ashamed to climb into the bed beside his wife. He did not trust
himself to not reach for her and ask for comfort he had not earned.

Sometime near dawn, exhaustion softened the edges of the room.
He fell asleep sitting upright, chin lowered, hands clasped loosely,
as if posture alone might count for repentance.

A soft voice drew him back.

"Eddie?"

He startled awake, blinking against the fog of sleep.

Lucy was sitting up, the blanket gathered around her. Confusion
flickered across her face, followed by tenderness, and something
else he could not yet name. It was fragile and expectant, and it fed
the small morsel of hope he still had.

"You slept in that chair all night?" she asked.

He rubbed a hand over his face. "I was afraid if I left, you'd disappear," he answered quietly.

She studied him for a long moment. Her eyes were puffy. He knew his must be the same.

"I want to be here," he said, the words scraping their way out, as he sat forward and reached for her hand. "Not just in this room. I want us to feel right again, Lucy, but I don't know how to get there."

Her breath wavered, but her gaze stayed steady.

"I don't need us to go back," she said. "We can't rebuild by pretending things look the same as before. I need to know you won't run when things get hard and that you choose us each and every time. Can you do that for me?"

Eddie nodded fiercely as he pumped her hand.

"We can't keep building our marriage on silence," Lucy continued. "But if you're willing to try, so am I."

Shame hit him sharp and familiar. Beneath it, resolve took shape. It was not peace, at least not yet, but an opening that felt honest and unavoidable.

He closed his eyes. "I wasn't honest," he said. "When you asked if I loved Elinor."

Lucy inhaled sharply.

"I don't love her," he said, quickly now. "I loved her in college. That was years ago. When she came to Croft Beach, I liked how she made me feel—needed, admired. And I regret letting that matter more than it ever should have."

He swallowed, steadying himself.

"Instead of drawing a line, I waited. I told myself silence was kindness. That restraint was faithfulness."

The words hung between them, stark and unsoftened.

Lucy nodded once. "Thank you for telling the truth."

Her quiet acknowledgment cut deeper than anger. He found himself wishing she would raise her voice or cry or break something. Anything would have been easier than the calm honesty she offered instead.

She pushed the blanket aside and stood.

"I'm going to make breakfast," she said gently. "You're welcome to join me. Or not."

She stepped into the hallway. Morning light wrapped around her, outlining the woman he loved and the life he had nearly lost. In that moment, Eddie saw the choice ahead of him as clearly as a line drawn across the floor. One path led back to hiding. The other demanded truth, spoken fully, even when it cost him.

He stood and followed her.

Sensibility had carried him into silence and fear. He could not keep calling that restraint when it was cowardice. If he wanted his marriage, his family, and the man he was still called to become, he would have to choose honesty again and again, in small moments and costly ones alike.

This morning, he took the first step.

He prayed for the courage to keep choosing it.

Chapter Nineteen

Rick woke before dawn with his heart pounding, the remnants of a nightmare clinging stubbornly to him. For a disoriented moment, Rick could feel the cold metal at his throat again—the weight of it, the way it stole his breath and sent panic flooding through his body.

He forced himself to lie still. The room was warm and familiar. The chain was not there. He was not underground. He breathed slowly until the pressure eased from his chest and the truth settled back into place.

Scrubbing both hands over his face and let out a shaky breath, Rick willed the last echo of fear to drain from his muscles. The gentle sounds of the house comforted and steadied him in a way only home could. Then the mattress shifted beside him, ever so slightly, followed by a small, sticky palm pressing against his cheek.

"Daddy?"

Ellie's whisper pulled him the rest of the way back into the present. He opened one eye and found her kneeling beside the bed in her pajamas, curls wild in every direction. Quackers was tucked under one arm and Flippers under the other, as if they had accompanied her on an important mission. Her expression was solemn with purpose.

"Daddy," she whispered. "My milk fell."

A soft, incredulous smile tugged at his lips. In the basement, he had prayed there would be enough milk to last one more day when Ellie was an infant. Now at three-years-old she was waking him with the so-called severity of having knocked her milk cup over.

Ellie tugged him toward the hallway with her slippery hands. The kitchen glowed in the early light. Maggie was already there, kneeling on the tile with a wad of paper towels, dabbing carefully at a small white puddle near the table.

"Morning, Brother Rick. I'm cleaning it," Maggie said, glancing up. "She bumped her cup."

Ellie hovered at Rick's side, fingers curled into the hem of his shirt. Her voice was barely above a whisper. "I spilled it."

Rick crouched in front of her at once. "That's okay, Little Love."

She studied his face. "Can I have more?"

"Yes," he said gently. "That shouldn't be a problem."

The tension in her shoulders eased, though she didn't move away just yet.

With a smile, Rick took the empty cup and carried it to the sink. He rinsed it, dried it, and opened the refrigerator. The milk carton sat heavy and full on the shelf.

He poured Ellie a fresh cup and set it in front of her. "Here you go."

She climbed into her chair and wrapped both hands around it. "Thank you, Daddy."

Maggie leaned against the counter. "Accidents don't count," she said with quiet certainty.

Rick smiled at her. "You're right. They don't."

Ellie took a careful sip, then looked up again. "You're not mad?"

"Not even a little," he said. "I'm glad you told me."

She nodded, satisfied, and returned to her cereal.

"So, where is everyone else?" Rick asked Maggie as he started the coffee maker.

She rattled the list off easily. "Walter is practicing his Bible verse for Sunday school. Sam is polishing his dress shoes for the wedding. Oh, and Lily is brushing her hair because she wants to look nice when my sister gets here."

Rick smiled. He couldn't be happier about how well Maggie had fit into their home—cheerful, confident, and treating his kids like siblings instead of cousins she was expected to tolerate.

"How's sharing a room with Lily going?" he asked.

"I love it." Maggie grinned. "She tells the best bedtime stories, like Daniel and the lions, and she lets me borrow her sparkly clips."

Before Rick could respond, a soft knock sounded at the doorway.

"Dad, she's here," Lily announced from the stairway as she ran down to open the door.

Marianne stepped inside carrying a couple of board games. Her dark jeans and cozy cardigan did little to hide the fatigue from her overnight shift, but she still somehow glowed. Rick knew relief was coming soon. A paramedic above her on the schedule had announced retirement, which meant Marianne would finally move to day shifts after the wedding.

"Morning, everyone," she said. "Did you miss me?"

The kids answered by launching themselves at her in a flurry of hugs and laughter. Rick hung back, smiling, content to wait his turn.

Watching them gather around her, all noise and joy and unfiltered affection, Rick felt gratitude bloom deep in his chest. Marianne brought steadiness to their lives. It was peace, the kind that didn't demand anything in return.

"Well," he said once the excitement settled, "do I get to kiss my queen now?"

Ellie gasped. "A queen!"

Marianne laughed. "Let's not rush to crowns. This queen feels more like a wicked stepmother in desperate need of coffee before I sprout a wart."

Rick grabbed for a second coffee mug as Marianne slipped in behind him, wrapping her arms around his waist. With a sigh, she rested her cheek between his shoulder blades. It lasted only a moment, but the warmth stayed with him even after she took the mug from his hands.

"You okay?" she asked softly.

"I am."

"You look rested."

"I slept."

Surprise softened her face. "Really, you did?"

He nodded, happiness pressing close, but he kept the moment quiet with the kids nearby. While Marianne sipped her coffee and chatted with her sister, Rick took Ellie into the bathroom and gently brushed her hair.

"Now Daddy will kiss you," Lily announced proudly when Marianne joined them in the den, looking far more human after having had caffeine. "You're the queen now and not the wicked stepmother."

Marianne went bright red as Rick nearly choked on his coffee. The children's laughter rang out, and the simplicity of the moment struck him hard. This was his life now. A life he had once believed was beyond reach.

After the kiss—enthusiastically applauded by their audience—Rick herded everyone into the SUV. The older kids barely waited for the engine to stop when they reached the church before scrambling out.

"Hey," Rick called as they tumbled onto the sidewalk, "who loves you more than all the sand on the beach?"

"You do!" four voices shouted.

"And God," Ellie added solemnly.

Rick laughed as he lifted her from her car seat and she kissed his cheek. On the sidewalk, Marianne and Maggie watched him with matching smiles.

As the boys raced ahead with Ellie chasing after them, Lily lingered. Her eyes were older than her years as she studied his face.

"You happy, Dad?" she asked.

"I am, Sweetheart. You?"

She nodded. "We're safe."

The words hit him hard as he squeezed her hand. "I know."

Lily smiled matter-of-factly, took Maggie's hand, and the girls dashed off to catch up with the others. Rick watched them disappear through the church doors as a memory rose, uninvited.

On their first Sunday at Croft Beach Community Church, Lily had stood just inside the sanctuary doors, her fingers clenched white around the handle of her cane and the sleeve of his jacket. She had hated the cane—hated how it made her feel exposed. She was so uncomfortable and nervous that she would not meet anyone's eyes.

He could remember her asking what would happen if he were not there when she came back. The question had gutted him. He recalled kneeling in front of her, hands steady on her shoulders. He had lowered his voice until it belonged only to them and then promising that he would be right there and that she would not be alone.

Pastor Fanny had entered the moment with quiet grace, kneeling to Lily's level, offering songs, a craft, and a seat saved just for her in Sunday school. Then Walter had stepped forward, flanked by his younger siblings, certainty written across his face.

Rick swallowed as the memory settled, tender and heavy. Lily had walked away that day with her siblings beside her, cane tapping softly against the floor, courage stitched together by love and promises kept.

He was grateful for the healing that had taken root slowly and held fast. More than anything, he prayed it would keep growing—through ordinary mornings, spilled milk, and all the small mercies still ahead.

Chapter Twenty

Lucy had woken before dawn sick again, curled on her side, one hand over her stomach and the other gripping the edge of the mattress. Eddie sat beside her, rubbing her back as she leaned over the pan he had placed on the floor, wishing he knew how to help.

By the time the sun came up, she was propped against the pillows with a cool cloth on her forehead, breathing carefully, her face pale and drawn.

"You should have gone to church," she whispered once the nausea eased. "I'm sure Ned could have used your help."

"Ned's got everything handled," he replied quickly. "I'm not going anywhere this morning."

She did not argue, something which he took as encouraging. But despite the progress they had made, Eddie felt helpless as he stepped into the kitchen. Doing nothing felt like the worst and so he busied himself by filling the kettle, even though his hands shook more than he wanted to admit.

Around four that morning, unable to sleep, he had searched for remedies on his phone, scrolling through article after article in the glow of the bathroom light. Ginger tea with a touch of honey was the one suggestion he kept coming back to.

He found a mug, added the teabag he had gone out to buy, and waited as the kettle began to hum. Each small motion reminded him how late he was to learning. As much as he wanted to kick himself for the ways he'd failed Lucy, he purposefully focused on preparing the tea instead of trying to keep a positive mindset.

"I read that ginger can help with the nausea," he said gently as he brought the mug into the bedroom. "I thought it might make the morning easier."

Lucy looked at the cup first, then up at him. The tightness in her expression eased, just enough to make the early-morning dash to the store feel entirely worthwhile. She accepted the mug with both hands and breathed in the warm scent of ginger and honey.

"Thank you," she murmured.

Eddie lingered, hands hovering uselessly at his sides, waiting to see if it helped—if he had done something right. As Lucy finished her tea, he texted Darcy to say he would be late but still coming. Then he turned back toward the woman he loved.

"Lucy, I told Darcy I'd meet him for lunch," he said. "But if you want me to stay, I can cancel."

For a moment, he hoped she would ask him not to go. Instead, she opened her eyes and met his with her familiar, steady calm, then turned her face away, shielding her thoughts from his searching gaze.

"Go," she urged gently. "You could use the fellowship. And yes, it's cliché, but you probably need time with Darcy now more than ever."

"You're sure?"

"Yes," she whispered. "Just come back afterward."

He nodded, the words settling in him like an anchor, and bent to squeeze her fingers. "I will. I promise."

She squeezed back, then let go. "And don't apologize for going. You've done enough apologizing. Just keep choosing us."

He nodded once. "I'm trying."

"I know," she said, softer this time. "Now go."

He brushed a strand of hair from her forehead, unable to stop himself. She did not flinch. Instead, a small smile touched her lips as her eyes fluttered closed.

He slipped out of the room quietly, carrying the empty mug with him so the scent of tea would not linger while she slept. In the kitchen, he allowed himself one long breath. His chest still felt raw, but not in the hollow, hopeless way it had earlier this month.

The five-minute drive to the marina felt both too long and not long enough. By the time Eddie reached the café, the sun had burned through the last of the morning haze. Families wandered past with strollers and dripping ice-cream cones, their laughter drifting on the salt air in a way that lately had been leaving him hollow. Today, it only made him restless and aware of how much he wanted to hold on to the good moments while they lasted.

Darcy was already seated, sunglasses pushed into his hair, studying the menu with the focus of a man reviewing a legal contract. He looked up the moment Eddie arrived, his gaze sharp and assessing.

"You made it," Darcy said, calm and even. "Good. Sit."

Eddie slid into the chair, half amused by the way Darcy scanned the patio as if cataloging exits and variables.

Rick crossed the patio a moment later, nodding to a few familiar faces before dropping into the empty chair. He gave Eddie's arm a brief, firm squeeze. "You look better," he said, not casually. "Lighter."

Eddie huffed a quiet laugh. "That obvious?"

"To us?" Rick said. "Yeah."

Darcy tilted his head, studying him. "You're still tired," he observed. "But you're not spiraling."

Eddie let out a slow breath. "I'm trying not to," he said honestly. "I'm staying focused. One thing at a time." He paused, then added, "I know I've got a long way to go."

Rick nodded, satisfied with the answer. "That's all anyone can ask."

Darcy pushed a menu toward Eddie. "You still need to eat. That part is non-negotiable."

Eddie smiled faintly. "Lucy wasn't feeling great this morning."

Darcy's expression softened in that way only people close to him ever noticed. "Morning sickness?"

"Yeah," Eddie said. "Apparently ginger is a miracle root."

Rick leaned back. "I didn't even know what morning sickness was back when I was in the cellar," he said bluntly. "But if it would've kept Louisa upstairs for even one day, I would've prayed for it."

When neither Eddie nor Darcy said anything in reply, Rick shrugged and reached for a roll. "Just calling it what it is."

Eddie stared down at the menu, then spoke again, voice steady but unguarded. "I went out to the shops and got some ginger tea and

Lucy thanked me. I know it seems like a small thing but considering everything we've gone through, it made me smile. In fact, she told me to stop apologizing and start showing up." He swallowed. "So that's what I'm trying to do."

Darcy tapped the table once. "Then you're on the right track."

Rick lifted his water glass. "To staying in the moment."

The server arrived, and Darcy ordered lobster Benedict without a glance at the price. Rick chose a chef's salad, while Eddie, after far too much deliberation, settled on avocado toast and hoped his stomach would cooperate.

His phone buzzed before he could hand the menu back.

Resting now. Thank you.

Lucy

Eddie exhaled, the tension easing out of his shoulders. He sent back a smiling emoji and slipped the phone into his pocket.

Darcy raised a brow. "Good news?"

"Yeah," Eddie confirmed. "I'm not fixed. I'm not there yet." He met their eyes. "But today feels… possible."

Rick lifted his glass again. "That's enough for now."

Darcy echoed the gesture.

Eddie joined them, the weight in his chest no longer failure but rather the fragile outline of hope. For today, he would hold on to that.

Chapter Twenty-One

Peace does not mean the past stops knocking. It means I decide which doors no longer open.

Rick balanced the cupcake carefully as he padded up the stairs. The house was quiet except for the soft hum of the refrigerator and the distant hush of the ocean beyond the windows.

Lily's door was cracked open. Rick nudged it wider with his shoulder and stepped inside, Daniel slipping in at his heels with a soft, hopeful whine.

She was sprawled across her bed, her stuffed lion tucked under one arm, hair fanned across the pillow. Daniel padded closer and settled beside her, resting his chin on the mattress as if he, too, wanted to wish her a happy birthday.

Rick paused for a moment, just watching her breathe. Ten years old. Somehow.

"Hey," he whispered. "Birthday girl."

Her eyes fluttered open, unfocused at first. Then she saw the cupcake.

Her gasp was immediate and joyful. "Dad!"

"Happy birthday, Sweetheart," he said softly. "Make a wish."

She pushed herself upright, blinking hard as if she wasn't sure she was fully awake. Rick set the cupcake on her bedside table and lit the candle. The tiny flame wobbled, then steadied.

Lily closed her eyes, lips moving silently, then blew. The candle went out in a curl of smoke.

"What did you wish for?" he asked.

She grinned. "Can't tell. It won't work."

"Smart girl."

She leaned forward and wrapped her arms around his neck, squeezing tight. Rick held her for a long second, pressing his cheek to her hair, letting the moment root itself where it belonged.

"Is today the day?" she asked, pulling back to pet Daniel. "The real day?"

"It is," he said. "Marianne texted me to say happy birthday from her and Maggie and Elinor. They promise to take good care of Daniel when we're gone."

Her smile softened, something calm and certain settling over her face. "Good."

Footsteps thudded down the hall, followed by Walter's unmistakable whisper-shout. "Is it time yet?"

Rick laughed. "You want to tell them, or should I?"

Lily slid out of bed, already buzzing. "I'll tell them."

She bolted for the door, cupcake forgotten for the moment.

Rick picked it up carefully and followed her into the morning.

They were out the door faster than Rick had dared hope. Shoes were pulled on crooked, sweatshirts tied around waists, backpacks double-checked and slung over shoulders. Soon, the SUV filled with chatter and the unmistakable rustle of anticipation.

The freeway was still mercifully light. Walter and Sam narrated every billboard as if it were a personal challenge. Ellie fell asleep again before they reached the on-ramp, her stuffed duck pressed to her cheek, curls escaping her ponytail with each soft breath.

The birthday girl watched the sun rise through the windshield, quiet in a way that felt thoughtful rather than afraid. Rick adjusted the rearview mirror and caught her eyes for a moment. She smiled at him—small, steady, unburdened—and turned back to the window.

Traffic thickened as they neared the exit for Disneyland. Rick followed the signs to enter the parking lot without second-guessing himself, hands relaxed on the wheel, heart steady.

They rolled into the parking lot and joined the slow, orderly lines, Cast Members waving them forward with practiced cheer. Rick shut off the engine and sat for a beat, taking in the sound of his children's voices overlapping, the smell of sunscreen and morning air, and the weight of the day ahead.

"Okay," he said, turning to face them. "Who's ready for an amazing birthday celebration for Lily?"

"Me!" All the children screamed and started giggling in unison.

They made it through security with Sam practically vibrating as the stroller got its routine check. Soon they were boarding the bus toward the park, each kid with their face pressed against the window. Music swelled around them, familiar and bright. When the doors whooshed open, they were swept into the crowd headed toward the front entrance and onto Main Street, U.S.A.

Rick stepped out with the kids and felt everything inside him soften. This time he wasn't the broken man fighting for breath while the crowds pressed in. He wasn't the father wondering if he would ever be enough. Today he was simply Dad, and he had come to give his kids a day that would feel like light.

Sam tugged at his sleeve. "Dad, why don't we get to skip the lines like we did with Uncle Darcy?"

Rick took the hit without letting it show on his face. The question landed hard, straight in the gut, because it wasn't really about lines. It was about money, about what he could and could not afford.

"Uncle Darcy has been very generous," he said gently. "But today is my gift to you all for Lily's birthday, and I can't afford the fast passes. So today we're standing in the regular lines. Think you can handle that?"

Walter frowned. "Is Uncle Darcy rich?"

"Very," Rick replied with a snort.

Sam gasped dramatically as he spotted the wait time board. "I think I'll die if I have to wait thirty minutes for that flying elephant ride Ellie likes."

Rick couldn't help laughing. "If you die, you'll ruin your sister's birthday."

Lily groaned. "Uh oh."

"We could play Queue Crew," Rick announced, inspiration striking.

Loving games, Sam perked up immediately. "What's Queue Crew?"

Rick explained the rules as though he hadn't invented them five seconds earlier. "One person picks a theme, such as princesses, superheroes, or animals, and everyone takes turns naming something they see that fits. No repeats. If you stall longer than three seconds, you're out."

Ellie gasped. "Three? That's impossible!"

He bopped her nose. "You'll dominate, Little Love."

And she did exactly that.

By late morning they were having so much fun that no one even mentioned the lines, which were thankfully short in the off-season.

At 11:45 they reached Toontown. The last time they'd been there, Lily wouldn't stop looking over her shoulder at him, clinging to his hand, terrified he might disappear in the crowd. Today she sprinted toward the grassy knoll with Walter and Sam close behind, yelling about no tag backs.

Rick did not chase; he just watched. His children were running, wild and unafraid.

Ellie tugged his sleeve. "Daddy, I'm hungry."

Rick slid off the backpack, and together they found a bright patch of fake grass between Mickey Mouse and Minnie Mouse's houses.

He unpacked sandwiches and fruit, laying everything out on a tea towel he'd thought to pack, while the older kids ran circles around them.

When the others eventually came racing back, flushed and laughing, they prayed quickly and ate slowly, surrounded by families just as happy as they were. After lunch, the older kids made a beeline for the cartoon dog pound. Ellie stayed and crawled into Rick's lap, curled under his chin, and fell asleep within seconds.

Rick did not move as her small body pressed against his. Her trust was the sweetest gift she could give him. He lowered his face into her curls and let himself cry quiet tears that felt like the glue sealing a wound shut.

"You'll never go back to the dark," he whispered.

Across the lawn Walter called, "Dad! Dad! Look at me!"

Rick wiped his face and lifted his hand in a wave. "I'm watching, buddy."

He was watching, and he always would be.

Ellie slept for almost an hour. Somewhere in that stretch, Lily wandered over and plopped down at his side, her whole face lit with contentment.

"She trusts you," she said simply.

He kissed her cheek. "I'm learning to trust me too."

Lily smiled and leaned against him, and Rick rested his cheek on her hair.

By six o'clock they had ridden almost every attraction the kids were tall enough for and were overflowing with stories and pride. After the wild west roller coaster, especially, Walter puffed out his chest and declared he was destined to be a roller coaster tester when he grew up.

They stayed through sunset and watched the flag retreat before Rick treated them to one last carton of fresh-popped popcorn for the walk back to the bus. As they headed toward the parking lot, Lily slipped her hand into his, not out of fear, but out of love.

They arrived home tired, sun flushed, sticky, and gloriously happy. Rick carried a sleeping Ellie inside and smiled when he saw Marianne and Maggie waiting in the living room. He laid Ellie gently beside Maggie, who stroked her curls while Daniel slobbered enthusiastic greetings all over the other kids.

Lily bent down and kissed Ellie's forehead. "Today felt like a promise," she whispered.

Rick's chest ached in the best possible way. "It was," he said softly.

He did not mean Disneyland; he meant fatherhood, and he meant forever.

After the kids were settling down upstairs and Marianne headed home for the night, Rick took one last peek around the house. A nightlight glowed in the hallway outside the bedrooms. He checked each door once more out of habit, then headed downstairs to the kitchen where the mail sat in a thin, crooked stack.

It was mostly all junk including a flyer about the new pizza restaurant opening up. There were unfortunately also a few bills he recognized. But then he saw the envelope.

His name was typed, not handwritten. The return address read Louisa.

Louisa.

Rick stood still at the counter, the hum of the house drifting around him as the children brushed teeth and changed into their pajamas.

Rick looked down at the envelope again.

His chest tightened, but it did not seize up. His hands stayed steady. The letter did not feel heavy so much as misplaced, like something that had been delivered to the wrong life.

He did not open it. He did not need to.

Rick set the envelope on the counter and took a slow breath, grounding himself in the ordinary chaos of the house. He could hear Lily shouting something triumphant about losing another tooth.

This was not a decision that required urgency, fear, or a phone call.

He folded the envelope once and walked to the kitchen recycle can. He lifted the lid and dropped it in. The paper slid down without resistance, landing atop wrapping paper scraps and empty juice boxes.

Rick closed the lid and calmly washed his hands at the sink, the warm water grounding him further, then dried them on a towel.

"Dad!" Lily called from the staircase. "I lost another tooth!"

Rick smiled and stepped back into the noise of the life that had chosen him back.

Louisa did not follow him in.

She did not get the day.

And Rick did not look back.

Chapter Twenty-Two

Eddie drove with the windows cracked, salt air slipping into the car in slow, steady waves. He hadn't turned on the radio. Silence felt less heavy this morning—cleaner somehow, like space instead of absence.

Things were getting better with Lucy. Nothing was permanently fixed nor finished yet. But there was no denying the forward motion.

He'd started thinking of their momentum as two steps forward and one step back. It was not failure, he had to constantly remind himself, but just motion.

He said it aloud, testing the truth of it. "Two steps forward," he murmured, then exhaled. "One step back."

The words steadied him because they were honest. They left room for effort without demanding perfection.

He thought of the scene from earlier that morning in the kitchen. Lucy had been standing at the counter, pale but determined, one hand braced against the edge as if willpower alone could keep her upright. He'd been surprised by the way she had watched him make the tea. Her expression had neither been wary nor hopeful. Instead, it had been accepting and that in itself made Eddie want to shout for joy.

Lost in thought, Eddie sped along the coastal road as a neighboring town came into view. At a red light, he rested his hands on the wheel and spoke quietly in the safety of the car.

"I don't know how to do this perfectly, Lord," he said. "But I'm doing it."

The admission felt steadier than a plea. He continued anyway, voice low and unguarded. "I want to be brave without pretending I'm not afraid. I want to stay."

The light turned green. He drove on, rolling the window down farther and letting the ocean air rush through the car.

The trick, he was learning, wasn't pretending that the fear wasn't there. It was choosing to move forward with it.

Movement ahead caught his eye. A couple stepped into the crosswalk.

They were young, likely in their early twenties, maybe. The woman wore an oversized sweater, her hand tucked into the crook of the man's arm. Her other hand rested on the unmistakable curve of her belly. The man leaned in as they crossed, his face open with a kind of unfiltered joy that stopped Eddie cold.

"Did you feel that?" the man said, his voice carrying through Eddie's open window. "I swear she just kicked."

The woman laughed. "You say that every time."

"Because every time it feels like a miracle."

They disappeared into a small storefront just beyond the crosswalk. Eddie's foot hovered over the brake a moment longer than necessary. Before he could talk himself out of it, he pulled into the nearest open space.

The sign above the shop read *Sweet Pea Baby & Co.* Pastel bunting fluttered in the breeze. Through the window, he could see that shelves were lined with impossibly small things. The store had everything from tiny socks and knit hats to blankets folded with care.

"I should head home," he said aloud, but his hand was already on the door.

Inside, he felt awkward at first, like a man stepping into a future still learning his shape. A woman behind the counter smiled warmly.

"Shopping for someone special?"

"My wife," Eddie said. "She's pregnant."

The words landed with unexpected ease.

He moved slowly through the shop, hands loosening at his sides as he went. He noticed the intention behind the displays. There was care and quiet hope stitched into every corner. Someone had imagined families like his when they'd built this place.

He picked up a pair of pale-yellow booties and turned them over in his palm. They were impossibly soft.

Their child would wear something like this. The thought no longer frightened him. It anchored him.

He brought the booties and an accompanying cap to the counter. A blanket printed with tiny stars caught his eye next. He plucked it off the display at once and added that to his growing pile of goodies.

Back in the car, he placed the small white bag on the passenger seat and buckled it in without thinking. The click of the seat belt sounded final in the best way.

He rested his forehead briefly against the steering wheel and breathed in deliberately until the ache in his chest softened into something workable.

Music drifted through the open air when he pulled into the driveway. Lucy was in the garden, kneeling near the rosemary bush, humming softly. Dirt smudged her palms. The speaker he'd bought her years ago played beside her phone.

She looked up when he approached and genuinely smiled.

"You're back," she said.

"I said I would be."

He held out the bag. "I saw something and thought of you. Of us."

She opened it carefully. When she saw the booties and hat, her breath caught. She didn't speak right away. She just held them.

"These are perfect," she said finally.

Eddie crouched beside her. "I don't want to miss this," he said. "Any of it. Even the hard parts."

Lucy set the booties gently beside the rosemary and reached for his hand, dirt and all. "Then stay," she said. "That's all I'm asking."

He stayed.

They sat shoulder to shoulder, the music drifting, the garden quiet around them. It wasn't resolution, but it was movement.

And for Eddie, that finally felt like progress he could trust.

Chapter Twenty-Three

Rick set six chairs in the living room, the way he did every week. Sunlight pooled across the rug, soft and warm, and the ocean breeze rattled the back screen door. Four chairs were for the kids, one for him, and one for whichever Bertram arrived to guide them.

Fanny came this morning, slipping in with a bag of still-warm donuts and a smile. The children greeted her eagerly. Ellie climbed onto Rick's lap with Quackers tucked under her arm, pressing her cheek to his chest as if she already sensed the weight hanging in the air.

Sam was the one who finally broke the quiet. "Where's Pastor Eddie? We haven't seen him in forever."

Fanny stroked Sam's hair. "Pastor Eddie asked for some time to rest," she said gently. "Sometimes grown-ups need help before they can help anyone else."

Sam grabbed her hand and looked up, worry edging his voice. "Did he do something wrong?"

Rick leaned forward, elbows braced on his knees. "No, buddy. He's just going through a lot right now."

Sam's mouth trembled. Rick recognized the sign immediately but before he could say anything, Walter sneaked in and cleared his throat softly. "It's like after we saw Mom last summer."

Sam stiffened, eyes darting toward his brother, but Walter didn't retreat. He leaned forward, jaw clenched with remembered fury.

"I didn't want to talk either," Walter said quietly. "I didn't want Dad to know what she said. Or how it felt."

Lily's hands curled into fists in her lap. "She lied about everything," she said fiercely. "She hurt us and then acted like it didn't matter."

Rick laid a steady hand on her back. "Sweetheart, I know."

She shook her head, eyes bright. "She chained me. And she acted like that was fine." Her voice cracked. "I hate her."

"What she did was wrong," Rick said, pulling Lily closer and holding on.

Lily's breath shuddered as she leaned into him. Walter slid his hand into hers and held on.

Sam swallowed. "When we got home… after seeing Mom… I didn't talk because I didn't want Dad to think I believed her. Even for a second." He blinked hard. "She said he lied. That he was weak. That he only wanted us because he didn't have anyone else."

Rick shifted Ellie to one knee and reached out with his free hand until his palm rested on Sam's shoulder. "Look at me, buddy."

Sam hesitated, then lifted his gaze.

Rick kept his voice steady even as his throat burned. "What she said was cruel. And false." He waited until Sam looked back at him. "You were a kid who wanted his mom."

Sam's eyes filled. "But I did believe her. For a minute. She's my mom."

"Yes, she is," Rick said gently. "And I will always be grateful that Louisa gave birth to you and gave you a chance at a normal childhood before we were reunited. But the most important thing to remember right now is this: even if you believed her—and you were allowed to—you also came home." His voice softened. "You came home and let me love you. That took strength."

Sam's breath shook. "I don't want Pastor Eddie to feel like I did. Alone."

Rick nodded slowly. "He doesn't want you carrying his pain, son."

Walter looked between them, then straightened. "Maybe we could tell him he isn't alone. The way you told us."

Rick blinked hard. For a moment, words wouldn't come.

"What a beautiful idea," Fanny agreed. "Words of compassion are never wasted."

The room settled into a soft, warm stillness. Ellie broke it with the certainty only a toddler could bring. "Daddy is a hero," she announced sleepily.

Walter snorted. "We already knew that."

Sam slid off his chair and climbed onto Rick's crowded lap, leaning back against him the way he hadn't in months. Rick wrapped both arms around him without thinking, pressing a kiss into his hair.

"You called me a superhero at Disneyland in July," Rick murmured. "Do you remember?"

Sam nodded. "I meant it."

Walter added, "Yeah, but you don't have to win games to be our hero, Dad."

Rick exhaled slowly, the breath leaving him all at once. He rested his cheek against Sam's hair and held him closer.

"You kids helped save me more than you know," he said.

Ellie curled tighter against him, wrapping her arms around Sam. Quackers slipped to the floor, forgotten. Walter and Lily leaned in from either side, their heads settling against Rick's shoulders until he was surrounded by the children who had survived so much with him.

When Rick looked up, Fanny was pocketing her phone, watching them with tears in her eyes.

Rick closed his eyes for a moment. His heart, once fractured, was being held together by four small bodies pressed close.

He looked around the circle.

"This is our family," he said. "And we're going to keep choosing each other."

Walter nodded fiercely. Sam stayed close. Lily wiped her eyes with the back of her hand. Ellie hummed against Rick's neck.

Rick felt whole in a way that deepened everything he had already reclaimed. The light through the window felt less like morning and more like a promise.

Chapter Twenty-Four

Eddie paused in the bedroom doorway, his eyes drawn to the prenatal appointment card Lucy had left on his nightstand. He was confident that she had placed it there deliberately, angled so he would see it when he woke. He was surprised, though, that she had not mentioned it again or asked whether he planned to come along. She had simply set it down and trusted him to decide.

The quiet weight of that choice pressed on him and so he picked up the card and read the details again, even though he had already memorized them. Tuesday. Nine-thirty. Dr. Davies. He folded the edge once between his fingers, then slipped it into his pocket instead of setting it back down. The motion felt deliberate, final.

Lucy stood in the kitchen, tying her hair back with careful fingers as the kettle warmed behind her. She looked pale but composed, her movements measured, as if she were conserving energy. When she saw him, she paused.

"You're up," she said softly.

"I want to come with you," he replied.

She studied his face for a moment, then nodded once and tossed him her set of car keys. "All right," she said. "Let's go."

The drive to the clinic passed in silence, but it was no longer the brittle quiet they had lived with since New Year's Eve. This silence felt tentative, even hopeful—something still forming. Eddie kept both hands on the wheel, though the impulse to reach for Lucy's hand stayed with him the entire drive. He noticed, instead, that she sat angled slightly toward him, one hand resting loosely in her lap, breathing slow and steady.

He took that as a good sign—and let himself believe there was reason for hope.

At the clinic, Lucy checked in while Eddie stood beside her, his hands buried in his pockets. When the nurse called her name, Lucy rose first. Eddie followed without hesitation.

Inside the exam room, he hovered near the counter until Lucy touched the chair beside her. "You can sit," she murmured.

He did.

Dr. Davies entered a moment later, her bright red hair and warm smile filling the room with practiced ease. "Hello, Lucy. And Pastor Ferrars. It's nice to finally meet you."

"Eddie," he said quickly. "Just Eddie. I'm here today as a husband, and—hopefully—as a dad."

Lucy glanced at him, something soft crossing her expression before she looked away again.

The doctor asked routine questions. Fatigue. Nausea. Appetite. Eddie listened closely, storing each answer as if it mattered that he remember them later.

Then the ultrasound machine hummed to life.

Lucy lay back as the paper crinkled beneath her. The gel made her flinch, and Eddie braced one hand against the chair, his pulse loud in his ears. The wand moved. The screen flickered.

For a long, breath-held moment, there was nothing. Then suddenly a flash appeared, a tiny, insistent rhythm pulsing into view.

"There it is," Dr. Davies said gently. "A strong heartbeat."

Eddie's breath caught. Lucy turned her head toward him instead of the screen.

"What do you see?" she whispered.

He could not answer right away.

A memory surfaced instead.

A cramped café on Maple Street. Rain streaking the windows. The smell of burnt espresso thick in the air. Lucy standing at the counter, apologizing profusely as she tried to mop caramel from a table after knocking over his drink. He had laughed—not because it was funny, but because she was trying so hard to make it right.

"I swear," she had said, cheeks flushed, "I'm not normally this destructive."

"You've ruined one latte," he had replied. "I think we'll survive."

She had smiled then, the unguarded kind that slipped past effort. Later, she brushed a stray paper filter from his sleeve and joked about being an "accidental therapist," listening patiently as he talked too much and revealed too little. Even then, he had known her gentleness was not performative. It was simply who she was.

The memory dissolved as quickly as it came.

The heartbeat remained.

Lucy reached for him, tentative. Eddie met her halfway, their fingers intertwining on instinct. The sound filled the room, steady and undeniable.

As the doctor printed the image and explained next steps, Eddie heard only fragments of her words. His attention stayed with that rhythm he'd heard and with the way Lucy's hand remained in his.

Outside, sunlight washed the parking lot in pale gold. Eddie held the door as Lucy stepped through, tugging her sweater closer against the breeze.

"You haven't said anything," she said quietly.

"I'm still taking it in," he replied. "The miracle of it."

She looked at him, startled. "A miracle?"

"Yes," he said. "You and our baby are the two most important people in my world, and I want to show up for you every time."

Her breath wavered. She reached into her purse, pulled out the appointment card, and held it toward him. "Then maybe you can keep this," she said. "I'd like you there with me."

He took it carefully. "Thank you."

They drove home without filling the space between them, but this drive felt different. When they pulled into the driveway, Lucy went inside while Eddie stopped at the mailbox out of habit.

On top of the bills lay a bright envelope, its edges softened by many hands. Walter's bold scrawl stretched across the front. Sam's uneven smiley faces crowded one corner. Lily's careful hearts lined the bottom. Ellie's purple thumbprint stamped the corner like a seal.

For Pastor Eddie—We love you. Feel better soon.

He carried it inside.

Lucy turned when she saw the envelope. "What's that?"

He opened it slowly. Crayon colors spilled across the page. Three superheroes stood side by side, capes flying: Dad, Uncle Darcy, and Pastor Eddie. Beneath them were simple messages.

We miss you.
Please feel better soon.
We love you.

Ellie's handprint filled the corner.

At the bottom, in Rick's steady handwriting: *You matter. You are not walking this alone.*

Lucy covered her mouth. "Oh," she whispered.

Eddie felt the tears come before he could stop them.

Lucy traced the handprint with trembling fingers, then stepped close enough that her shoulder brushed his. "They really do love you," she said.

"I love them too," he replied. "And I'm trying. I really am."

She closed her eyes for a moment, then opened them again. "Come inside," she said. "Let's just be together today."

He followed her inside, the card still in his hand. The future no longer felt like something he had to outrun. Instead, it felt like something he could walk toward.

Eddie opened the calendar on the wall and wrote the next appointment in careful block letters. He capped the pen and couldn't resist a smile.

Chapter Twenty-Five

Rick's Journal

My body still listens to shadows.

I am afraid of ruining everything I love with a fear I cannot always control.

Rick woke choking, his body jolting upright before his mind could catch up with him.

For a disoriented second, he was back on concrete, the cold seeping into his shoulders, the metallic tang of bleach and rust clogging his throat. His heart hammered as if escape were still required, as if lying still were dangerous. He swung his legs over the side of the bed and staggered toward the bathroom, barely making it to the sink before retching.

When it passed, he gripped the counter with both hands and stared at his reflection. His face was pale, his eyes too bright, his breath shallow and uneven. Louisa's voice threaded through him, poison-sweet and sharp with command, the way it always did when his defenses were lowest.

Lie still. Good boy. No one will want you after what I've used.

"Stop," he whispered, pressing his palms hard against his eyes. "Please. Stop."

The terror did not vanish, but another voice cut through it, steady and sure.

Marianne's.

"Rick," she said gently. "Look at me."

He could hear the certainty in her voice, the way she always spoke when she was anchoring him.

"I trust you," she told him. "I chose you. And we will get through this together, one step at a time."

His chest tightened, not with panic this time, but with grief as he slid down the wall until he was sitting on the tile, knees drawn up, arms wrapped around himself.

"God," he choked. "Help me. Please don't let me hurt her."

He stayed there, breathing through the aftershocks, counting tiles, counting seconds. The house was quiet—too quiet.

He did not hear the door at first. Only when the air shifted did he realize he was not alone.

Darcy crouched a few feet away, hair rumpled, breath uneven as if he had come straight from sleep. He did not rush closer. He stayed where he was, letting Rick see him.

"I knocked for five minutes," Darcy said quietly. "When you didn't answer, I used my key."

Rick let out a sound that might have been a laugh if it had not broken halfway through.

Darcy waited.

"It's her," Rick said finally, staring at the floor. "It's always Louisa. I think I'm fine, and then—" He swallowed hard. "Marianne keeps telling me we'll figure things out together, but what if I freeze? Or panic? Or remember Louisa when Marianne touches me?"

He pressed his forehead to his knees. "What if I ruin everything?"

Rick's hand moved before he realized what he was doing. His phone was already in his palm, the screen lighting the tile.

Darcy noticed at once.

"Hey," he said, alert. "What are you doing?"

Rick swallowed. His thumb hovered over Marianne's name.

"I can't do this," he said quietly. "I don't see another way that doesn't end with me hurting her."

Darcy leaned back on his heels. "You're thinking about canceling the wedding."

Rick did not answer. He did not need to.

Darcy exhaled through his nose. "Okay. First, I need you to put the phone down."

Rick shook his head. "I'm not trying to run. I'm trying to protect her."

"I know," Darcy said. "That's the problem. Fear is making decisions it doesn't get to make."

He waited until Rick's grip loosened.

"Now listen to me," Darcy continued, quieter. "You don't solve fear by erasing the future. You solve it by telling yourself the truth."

Darcy shifted, then pulled Rick up and led him to the bed, where they sat.

"Look," he said, softer now. "I'm not saying this magically stops being hard."

Rick huffed a weak laugh. "That would have been nice."

"Yeah, well." Darcy glanced at him. "Life continues to ignore my preferences."

That earned a real—if shaky—smile.

Darcy went on. "Here's the part people don't say out loud. Sometimes the bravest thing isn't pushing through. It's stopping and saying, 'I need a minute.'"

Rick rubbed at his eyes. "I hate that that feels like failure."

"It's only failure if you pretend nothing's happening," Darcy said. He tilted his head. "You don't."

Rick did not answer, but his shoulders loosened.

Darcy nudged Rick's knee with his own. "If your brain starts misfiring, tell her. If your body locks up, stop and breathe. That's not ruining anything. That's you staying present."

Rick swallowed. "And if I don't get it right the first time?"

Darcy snorted softly. "Rick, you couldn't get the coffee maker right for six months after the rescue."

"That was different."

"No, it wasn't," Darcy said. "You learned and eventually the coffee maker was your friend and not the enemy."

Rick let out a breath that tipped into quiet laughter before dissolving into tears.

Darcy moved closer then, slow and deliberate, and rested a steady hand between Rick's shoulders. When Rick leaned into it, Darcy pulled him into a firm embrace, grounding him with the same fierce loyalty he had offered for decades.

"You're not dirty," Darcy murmured. "Not ruined. And Louisa didn't take intimacy from you. She used violence and lied about what it meant. That's not the same thing."

Rick trembled, but this time the shaking did not feel like drowning.

"You're not going to ruin anything," Darcy said. "You are allowed to stop when something feels wrong. Marianne will stop with you. She loves you for who you are, not for who you think you're supposed to be."

Rick's voice barely held together. "What if I remember Louisa when she touches me?"

Darcy did not answer right away. He shifted on the bed, and scrubbed a hand over his face as he clearly worked at choosing his words carefully.

"Rick," he said finally, quieter now, "Marianne's scared too."

Rick frowned, the panic faltering just enough to let confusion in. "She doesn't act like it."

"Think about it from her point of view." Darcy blushed as he continued. "She's a virgin. She's walking into intimacy for the first time with a man she loves who's been hurt in ways she can't predict or control. She knows you might freeze. She knows you might panic. She knows there are memories she can't compete with." He paused. "And she still chose you."

Rick's throat tightened. "I don't want to be the thing that scares her."

Darcy shook his head. "You're not."

Rick still looked unconvinced.

Darcy huffed a short breath. "For what it's worth, I was terrified on my honeymoon."

Rick blinked. "You?"

"Yes, me," Darcy said dryly. "Despite the confidence you may have noticed, I didn't know what I was doing. Trust me when I say that our wedding night was no cinematic masterpiece the first or even the second time we did it. We were fumbling and laughing and crying all over ourselves."

Darcy exhaled. "Loving someone doesn't magically make you competent."

Rick's throat tightened.

"Caroline trusted me anyway," Darcy said. "Not because I had it all figured out, but because I told her when I didn't. When I needed to stop. When I needed a minute."

Rick nodded slowly.

After a moment, Darcy stood and brushed his hands on his jeans.

"You okay enough to sleep?" he asked.

Rick nodded.

At the bedroom door, Darcy paused and looked back. "And Rick? If you tell anyone what I said about my honeymoon I will never forgive you."

Rick laughed as he threw a pillow at Darcy.

When the house fell quiet again, Rick lay back down. His body still ached. His throat still burned. But the darkness no longer felt absolute.

In a few days, he would marry the woman he loved. After Easter, he would stand in a science classroom, chalk dust on his hands, answering questions and looking forward instead of back. The fear had not vanished, but it no longer felt like a verdict.

He whispered into the quiet, "Help me trust joy."

And when he imagined God placing Marianne's hand in his— steady, patient—on their wedding day, the darkness no longer felt like something he had to face alone, and he fell asleep with a smile on his lips.

Chapter Twenty-Six

Text Message from Rick to Eddie

*If something needs to be said,
say it before the day gets loud.
Don't let regret talk louder than
you do.*

Eddie nearly knocked the vacuum into the coat rack as he dragged it backward out of the hallway.

"Come on," he muttered, catching it before it toppled. "You're not winning this."

The vacuum whined in protest as he wrestled the cord free from around the leg of the console table. He followed it into the living room, where half the couch cushions were stacked on the floor and a basket of unfolded laundry sat abandoned near the armchair. A faint smell of lemon cleaner lingered in the air, sharp and unfinished.

From the kitchen came the steady, unmistakable sound of chopping.

With a sigh, Eddie shut the vacuum off and leaned against the doorway. Lucy stood at the counter, shoulders squared, hair pulled back in a loose tie, knife moving with careful precision. The radio played softly near the window—something upbeat and old-fashioned, the kind of song she liked when she needed to keep going without thinking too hard.

"You don't have to finish that," he said.

She didn't turn. "I was in the middle of making dinner when you manhandled the vacuum from me."

"The doctor said you needed to take things easier," he tried to remind her. "Making a gourmet dinner, vacuuming, and folding laundry can't possibly be your definition of taking it easy. And reorganizing the bookshelf?"

She paused, the knife hovering. Then she frowned. "Those are my usual chores around here, Eddie. I can't just stop doing them because I'm pregnant. Women long before me have kept working right up until delivery."

"I know," he said gently. "And I know you are frustrated, love, but other women have had to be put on bed rest. You'd hate that even more, right?"

She finally looked at him, eyes tired but alert, as if measuring whether to argue. "You don't have to take over."

"I'm not trying to," he said. "I just want to help."

Her mouth twitched. "I've never seen anyone wrestle so much with a vacuum. It's actually very…entertaining."

"There you have it. If you care to sit yourself down, ma'am, it will be my honor to provide the entertainment."

That got a quiet laugh out of her. She set the knife down and stepped aside. "Fine. But if you burn dinner, I will not be held responsible if I go out and buy the fanciest steak in town."

"Threat noted, madam," he said solemnly in his poshest butler impersonation, as he playfully led her to the rocking chair by the window.

With a small groan of relief, she lowered herself carefully and let the chair move on its own momentum. Winking at his wife, Eddie dragged the vacuum back into the room. With an exaggerated bow, he began to hoover around the corners, narrowly missing the furniture. Her laughter as he made a fool of himself was a gift to his soul, and he couldn't stop smiling as he unplugged the cord and turned back to her. She had one hand resting over her stomach, fingers splayed as if marking time.

"You okay?" he asked.

"I am," she said. "Just… slower than I want to be."

He nodded. "That tracks."

She watched him for a moment as he filled a glass with water and set it beside her. "You don't usually notice this stuff."

He shrugged. "I'm trying to notice better."

Lucy tilted her head. "That sounds exhausting."

"Only because I've been bad at it," he said.

She smiled faintly. "You said it, not me."

He moved back into the living room, but instead of sitting on the couch, he knelt beside the rocking chair, settling on the rug with a wince.

"You don't need to sit on the floor," she said.

"I do," he replied.

"Why?"

He hesitated just long enough to make her curious, then leaned forward and rested his head against her stomach carefully and deliberately.

"Oh," Lucy breathed.

Her hand hovered for a moment before sliding into his hair, fingers gentle but certain. She rocked slowly, the chair creaking in rhythm with the radio.

"I don't know if you can hear me yet," Eddie spoke quietly. "But I figured I should say something."

Lucy swallowed. "You don't have to—"

"I want to," he said.

She nodded and let him continue.

"I'm Dad," he murmured. "Which feels… unreal to say out loud." He paused, choosing honesty over polish. "I'm not always great at this. I overthink. I freeze. I say the wrong thing."

Lucy smiled down at him as he continued. "But I'm here, little one. And I'm not planning on leaving because I love you and your mommy more than the moon itself."

The room felt very still around them as the music continued in the background and Eddie learned to appreciate this new variation of quiet in the house that felt more like a lullaby than any doomsday warning.

Lucy's voice trembled just slightly. "I've been waiting for that."

"For what?"

"For you to talk to the baby," she said. "It might seem silly to you, but you see it in the movies and read it in the paperbacks—those moments where the mom and dad are listening and talking to the baby. I've always… well, I guess I've always wanted that."

He lifted his head a little. "I want you to have everything you want. Okay?"

She nodded and he looked into her eyes bright with unshed tears. Lucy continued to rock, one hand steady in his hair. "This is all I need," she finally said, closing her eyes.

When he finally shifted, rubbing at his knees, she raised an eyebrow. "You ever regret breaking up with Elinor?"

"I regret nothing," he insisted, standing stiffly. "Except these old man joints."

She patted the couch beside her. "Come sit like a normal person."

They sat together for a while, talking about nothing in particular— the upcoming wedding, the garden, whether the baby would inherit Lucy's stubbornness or Eddie's inability to leave well enough alone. The afternoon stretched without urgency, held together by shared quiet.

Later, when Eddie stepped outside to water the plants, Lucy followed and settled on the bench near the rosemary, humming along with the music drifting from the open kitchen window. The scent of earth and herbs clung to the cooling air.

When he finished, he sat beside her. She took his hand and placed it over her belly.

"I don't know what comes next," she said.

He squeezed her fingers. "Neither do I."

She leaned into him. "But today feels good."

He agreed with a smile of contentment and kissed her gently on the lips.

The sun dipped lower, the air cooling around them. Eddie shifted closer, tugging a blanket high over her shoulders. When she rested her head against his shoulder, he stayed exactly where he was, and silenced his phone without even glancing at the display screen.

CHAPTER TWENTY-SEVEN

Rick's Journal

There was a time I believed no one would ever want the man I had become in the dark. But God keeps proving me wrong. Today I stood at the end of an aisle and watched a woman walk toward me with certainty in her eyes. Sometimes redemption looks like being chosen when you still fear you're unworthy.

Rick's knees felt steadier than he expected as he took his place beneath the white canopy Darcy and Caroline had borrowed from Jane Austen's Academy for the day. Morning sunlight filtered through the fabric, and crystals looped along the edges scattered soft prisms across the backyard. The air smelled faintly of ocean salt and eucalyptus from the wreaths Elinor had helped hang earlier that morning. His heart beat fast, but it felt alive. More importantly, he was free and about to marry the woman of his dreams.

Caroline stood to the left of Pastor Ned with Ellie perched on her hip, Quackers tucked neatly against her dress. Lily and Maggie stood beside them, proudly holding twin bouquets of wildflowers that matched the floral crowns all three girls wore in their hair. Walter and Sam flanked Rick, quiet but watchful, offering occasional nods of encouragement.

Darcy, in full best-man mode, adjusted his cufflinks with unnecessary precision before murmuring, "You're doing great. Just breathe."

Fanny nodded to someone near the speakers, and his favorite movement from Prokofiev's *Romeo and Juliet Suite No. 2* swelled through the yard. Guests rose to their feet. The canopy's sheer curtains fluttered open with the ocean breeze as Elinor and Marianne appeared at the back of the aisle. And Rick forgot how to breathe for a minute as he took in the vision she made.

Marianne walked alone toward him with the sunlight catching the pearls woven through her raven-black hair. Her empire-waisted satin dress moved like water as it skimmed past her feet, trailing softly behind her. Elinor followed a few steps behind in a pale pink dress, offering Rick a kind smile. But Rick truly had eyes for only one woman, and even the color of Elinor's dress barely registered.

Halfway down the aisle, Marianne paused and a proud Eddie stepped forward from the front row to offer his arm. He too grinned up at Rick and together they continued forward to where Rick waited. She must have seen Rick's love radiating from him because her own eyes shone with certainty—and something fierce beneath it.

Pastor Ned stepped forward, grinning, Bible open in his hands. His voice was warm as he welcomed everyone, though Rick barely heard the opening words. His focus had narrowed to the woman standing before him.

"Rick and Marianne have written their own vows," Ned announced. Rick chuckled, realizing he had missed a good ten to fifteen minutes of the ceremony while staring at Marianne like an idiot.

With a wink as if she knew what he was thinking, Marianne accepted her handwritten vows from Elinor and spoke.

"Rick," she began, her voice strong though emotion trembled beneath it, "when I first met you, I saw a man carrying more weight than any one person should have to bear. But I also saw the strength God placed in you; strength you didn't yet recognize. You love with courage. You father with tenderness. Today I vow to walk with you in every season of healing. I vow to remind you, whenever the shadows whisper otherwise, that you are worthy of love, joy, and belonging. I vow to choose you every day, the same way God has chosen us for this life together."

Rick swallowed hard. Darcy nudged his elbow in quiet encouragement.

Rick lifted Marianne's hands and kissed them before beginning.

"Marianne, you found me at a time when I believed any chance of happiness was gone. But you—Marianne Dashwood—you never asked me to be a different man. You didn't demand that I meet expectations or prove I was enough. You asked only that I be honest, present, and willing to trust that God had more for us than the memories I carried."

He drew a steadying breath, his voice thick as he looked into the dark brown eyes that had anchored him since the night she first appeared in that cellar, bringing hope he had not believed possible.

"You loved my children before you asked anything for yourself. You stood with me in fear, uncertainty, and hope. Today I vow to love you with a grateful heart, to listen when you speak, to stop when something hurts, and to build a home with you that reflects the grace God has shown us. I vow to choose joy with you, even when joy feels like the bravest choice we can make."

Marianne's eyes shimmered and unbidden Rick brushed a tear from her cheek.

Pastor Ned's voice thickened. "By the authority given to me by God and the State of California, I now pronounce you husband and wife. Marianne, you may kiss your groom."

With delighted shrieks from the crowd, Marianne threw her arms around Rick's neck, pulling him down toward her smiling face. Laughter rippled as she kissed him—loud, unreserved, joyful. Ellie squealed. Walter punched the air. Lily clung to Maggie's arm, hopping with excitement. Sam grinned as if his face could barely contain his joy.

Hand in hand, Rick and Marianne walked back up the aisle. Ellie broke free from Caroline and ran toward them, laughter ringing out as the other children followed, a tangle of arms and excitement encircling the newlyweds. Rick laughed too, the sound unfamiliar but welcome, and bent to gather them close as Marianne leaned into his side.

The backyard shifted into celebration as if on cue. Lanterns swayed overhead. The children ran barefoot in the sand beyond the fence flying a kite that Darcy had gifted them. Laughter rose like sunlight.

Marianne laughed softly from behind Rick during a lull in the activities. "Stop petting the furniture. We're really husband and wife, Mr. Wentworth. You're not asleep. I promise."

Chuckling, he looked into her sparkling eyes and thanked God yet again for this amazing woman—the one who had answered the priority one call from dispatch a year ago to the day.

As he swung her onto the hastily created dance floor, she rested her head on his shoulder, and he couldn't agree more with the crooner singing *The Way You Look Tonight* and found himself humming along.

"Are you all right?" she whispered.

"I'm better than all right," he murmured. "I didn't think joy could feel this perfect."

When the song ended, Darcy swooped in with a mischievous grin. "My turn."

Marianne laughed as she let him take over.

Lily tugged on Rick's sleeve. "Dad, it's our dance now."

Rick lifted her onto his shoes, and they spun beneath the lanterns. Walter and Sam waited nearby for their turns, eyes bright with anticipation.

Then Rick noticed Lucy.

She sat at a nearby table with Pastor Fanny. Her smile was faint, her color washed thin beneath the lantern light. One hand rested low on her abdomen, fingers curled protectively. Eddie hovered just behind her chair, one hand braced against the table, trying— and failing—to look calm.

Rick's unease sharpened. He had learned to trust that feeling. His body always knew before his mind caught up.

Lucy shifted, drawing in a shallow breath. "I—I feel dizzy."

Marianne was there instantly.

She crossed the space with swift, practiced purpose, her joy vanishing into focus as she knelt in front of Lucy. "Okay," she said calmly. "That's all right. Stay with me. Slow breaths, darling. In through your nose. Out through your mouth."

Lucy obeyed, though her breath trembled.

Rick stopped just behind Marianne, close enough to hear the even cadence of her voice, close enough to see Eddie's hands beginning to shake. He recognized the look on Eddie's face. There was the desperate need to *do something*, anything, paired with the terror of not knowing how.

Marianne's eyes moved quickly, cataloging Lucy's color and posture, the protective curve of her arm over her abdomen. "Are you having pain? Cramping? Any bleeding?"

Lucy swallowed hard. "Pain. It's low, and—it's getting worse." Her voice broke. "Marianne, I'm scared. What's going to happen to my baby?"

The word *baby* seemed to still the air around them.

Marianne nodded once, grounding them both. "Okay. We're not panicking. But we *are* going to the hospital. Right now."

Phones came out. Whispers rippled outward like waves. Someone said Marianne's name again, unnecessarily, as if needing reassurance that she was still there.

"Eddie," Marianne said, without looking up, her tone composed but firm. "I need you to listen."

He nodded too fast. "Yes. Just—just tell me what to do."

"I need you to go to the driveway and help direct the paramedics back here when they arrive. Can you do that for Lucy?"

Eddie hesitated, torn, his gaze flicking between Marianne and Lucy. Then Lucy reached for him.

"Please," she whispered. "Go."

That did it.

He nodded and rushed off with Darcy, shoulders tight, breath uneven.

With a quiet exhale, Marianne turned her full attention back to Lucy. "You're doing exactly what you should. Keep breathing with me."

Rick stepped closer, anchoring himself beside Lucy's chair in case Marianne needed him.

"I'll drive Eddie," he offered, already reaching for his car keys.

"No," Pastor Fanny said at once.

All eyes turned to her.

She stepped closer, placing a steady hand over Rick's. Her voice remained level, pastoral, unyielding. "I will drive. We don't want the bride and groom leaving the reception when they have a flight to catch in several hours."

Rick blinked, stunned. "I'd completely forgotten."

"Well, thankfully, I hadn't," Fanny said gently. "Ned already called emergency when it all started, so they should be here any moment.

And I'll take Eddie in my car. Don't you worry, Lucy. We'll be at the hospital when you're brought in."

As if on cue, the distant sound of sirens drifted in. A hush fell.

Someone murmured a prayer aloud. Others bowed their heads instinctively. Rick felt the weight of hands pressing briefly against his shoulder, his back—silent solidarity, faith moving without announcement.

Marianne glanced up and caught the eye of the lead paramedic. "Thank you, Fanny," she said, patting the older woman on the shoulder, then whispered to Rick, "Why don't you sit here with Lucy until they load her up?"

Seeing Marianne start talking in hushed tones to her co-workers, Rick crouched beside her chair as another wave of pain hit Lucy, who groaned softly, fingers tightening in the fabric of her dress.

He squeezed her shoulder, steady and sure. "You're not alone," Rick said steadily. "We're here, and help is already on the way."

Tears slipped free as Lucy nodded. "I'm sorry," she whispered. "I didn't want to ruin your wedding."

"You didn't ruin anything," Rick said firmly. "You listened to your body. That matters. Go take care of yourself, and we'll see you in Bath in a couple weeks. Okay?"

Lucy nodded again as the paramedics stepped forward, voices calm, and movements efficient. With a squeeze of the hand, Rick stepped back as Lucy was lifted gently onto the gurney and into the ambulance. He caught Eddie's eye just before the doors closed— fear written clear and raw across his face.

Rick held his gaze and nodded once, trying to convey his support. *You're not alone.*

Gravel crunched beneath the tires, then the taillights disappeared down the drive.

When Rick returned to the yard, Pastor Ned had already gathered family into a prayer circle. Rick stepped in beside Marianne, his pulse still racing beneath the calm he held in place.

Ned prayed softly but steadily for Lucy's body, for the child, for wisdom, and for peace over Eddie.

When he looked up, Ellie stood beside him clutching Quackers, solemn. Lily pressed close.

"Is Mrs. Lucy going to be okay?" Lily whispered.

"We're praying for that," Rick said, drawing her in.

"We'll pray extra hard," Sam added, slipping his hand into Rick's.

Rick closed his eyes. Marianne's arm was firm against his side, Ellie's small hand curled into his shirt, Sam's fingers laced through his own. The lights overhead swayed once in the evening breeze, and he stayed where he was, breathing until the pounding in his chest eased.

PART III

Rick's Journal

Somewhere in the quiet of this week, something shifted. I stopped bracing for the past and started reaching toward the future. Healing isn't a finish line; it's a direction. And I'm finally walking toward it with steady feet.

CHAPTER TWENTY-EIGHT

The hospital waiting room felt colder than any sanctuary Eddie had
ever preached in. The overhead lights buzzed with a tired, restless
hum, and the plastic chairs seemed designed more for endurance
than comfort. Darcy sat rigid on one side of him, his jaw clenched,
every muscle held too tightly. Ned sat on the other, his hands
loosely clasped between his knees, his head bowed in a quiet,
steady prayer that felt as though it were holding the room together
by threads.

Eddie could not still his hands. They were knotted together so
tightly that his knuckles ached. The imprint of Lucy's trembling
grip still burned across his palms. His mind replayed the moment
she had swayed at the wedding and the way her breath faltered as
she'd turned to Eddie with desperation and fear stark in her eyes.
Each memory layered itself over the last until breathing felt near
impossible.

Darcy finally exhaled, the sound sharp in the cold room. "We're
here," he said quietly. "Whatever happens, we're not leaving you."

Eddie nodded, though the motion felt unsteady. He did not trust
his voice. Fear had pooled in his throat over the last three hours.
His thoughts were sharp, metallic, and unforgiving. He had waited
for certainty when love had asked for courage. And now he feared
there was no moment left to step into.

The double doors opened and Lucy's obstetrician, Doctor Davies,
stepped inside with a chart tucked under her arm. Eddie recognized
the expression immediately and fell back down into his chair. The
doctor's eyes were too calm, too practiced, too gentle. It was the
expression he'd worn dozens of times when trying to offer comfort
to those who were grieving.

Shaking his head in a desperate need to see the doctor's expression in a different light, Eddie stood so quickly that the room tilted. Darcy's hand shot out, gripping his elbow before he could stumble.

"Mr. Ferrars," Doctor Davies said softly. "Thank you for waiting."

Eddie's pulse hammered in his ears. Did she really think he was going to leave? What other option did he have?

The doctor hesitated, then let her shoulders fall with quiet finality. "I am very sorry. We were not able to save the child."

The world did not crash or explode. Instead, it simply stopped, as though time itself had drawn a hard, merciless line—one he realized, with sickening clarity, he had crossed too late.

A sound escaped Eddie—raw and small, barely more than breath. His legs weakened beneath him, and Darcy's grip tightened, holding him upright when he could no longer remember how to stand. Ned moved closer, his hand settling between Eddie's shoulders, steady and grounding.

The doctor continued gently. "Physically, your wife is stable. She is with a nurse now. She is asking for you."

Eddie nodded once. The motion was barely more than a flinch, but it was all he could manage. "Take me to her," he whispered.

"I must warn you that she is in shock, but she needs you more than she probably even realizes at this moment."

Eddie stared unseeing at the doctor trying to understand her warning but just shook his head again and moved to follow her.

Darcy squeezed his shoulder. "Go. We'll be right here."

Ned murmured, "You are not walking through this alone."

Eddie barely heard them as he followed the doctor down the hallway that smelled of antiseptic and loss. Every step hurt. Every memory hurt more. Lucy laughing at breakfast that morning, Lucy guiding his hand to her stomach only hours earlier, Lucy whispering that the baby felt like bubbles inside her.

They stopped at a partially open door and he knew what was waiting for him on the other side and wanted to shout at the doctor to find him the exit. He wanted to scream at the smiling nurse who passed by for failing his wife and his child. He wanted most of all to run outside and never enter the room. He felt like such a coward. He had stood at a distance when he should have stood beside her, and now the cost of that hesitation pressed down on him with every step.

His feet didn't listen to his chaotic thoughts and somehow he found himself inside the hospital room.

Eddie glanced around and tried to take in the scene. Caroline sat on the edge of the bed with her arm wrapped around Lucy's shoulders, her braids falling forward like a curtain shielding Lucy from the world. Fanny stood near the foot of the bed, rubbing Lucy's feet as she bore witness to a grief she had shepherded too many families through.

Calling himself a coward, Eddie took a deep breath, stepped closer and got his first look at his wife.

Lucy was folded in on herself, both hands covering her face. Her shoulders shook with quiet, uncontrollable sobs. She looked small—too small—a woman built of faith and grit and gentleness, cracked straight down the center.

Caroline looked up first, her eyes softening with sorrow and strength. "Eddie…"

Lucy went still at the sound of his name. Slowly, painfully, she lifted her head.

Her eyes were swollen and red, her cheeks streaked with tears. Her mouth trembled as she tried, and failed, to hold herself together.

"You came," she whispered.

"Of course I came," he said, though his voice cracked anyway. "I've been outside in the waiting room for three hours, twenty six minutes, and—" Eddie glanced at his wristwatch – "forty-eight seconds. I could never have left."

Her gaze searched his face before dropping, hurt shadowing every fragile inch of her expression. "We had just started to reconcile. You spoke to the baby."

Eddie closed his eyes. "I know," he said, and the words tasted like ash. "That's what I can't stop thinking about. I waited until hope felt safe to me—and I should have been there for you so much earlier, when it was fragile."

Caroline shifted as if to give them space, but Lucy's hand shot out and gripped her sleeve with quiet desperation, freezing all three of them.

"Please stay," Lucy whispered. "Both of you."

Fanny moved closer and rested a steady palm on Lucy's calf in silent support.

Eddie approached the bed slowly terrified of how she might react. "May I sit?"

Lucy nodded, the motion barely perceptible.

He sat on the edge of the bed. His hands trembled as he reached for hers, open and gentle, asking rather than assuming.

She let him take them.

"You told me to rest at the wedding," she whispered. "You always say the right things too late."

Shame pressed hard against his ribs. "I am sorry," he said, the words breaking completely. "Not because I didn't care—but because I cared and still waited. I thought I had more time to be brave. I was wrong."

Her chin trembled.

Then her voice cracked, fragile and devastating. "He was ours… it was a boy."

Eddie bowed his head over her hands and kissed her wedding ring as a quiet, gutting sound shook him from the inside out.

"I loved him," he sobbed. "I loved him, Lucy—and I hate that he only knew the sound of my voice for a moment. He deserved more of me."

Her responding cry came like an unraveling, heartbreak and longing and something sacred wove them together as she leaned against him. She pressed her forehead to his shoulder, her fists twisting in his shirt. Their joint sobs broke through them in waves that felt too honest for the thin walls of the hospital room.

He wrapped both of his arms around her, holding her as if anchoring her there. "I'm not leaving," he whispered. "Not tonight. Not ever."

Her fingers tightened in his shirt as she looked up with misty eyes, and Eddie finally understood what Lucy had been asking of him all along.

She had never asked for distance to punish him. She had asked because she needed him to choose her fully—before hope was at risk, before love became an emergency.

Tonight—far too late for the child they had lost, but not too late for the life still before them—Eddie finally understood that being present was not something you waited to feel ready for. It was something you chose, even when it terrified you.

Chapter Twenty-Nine

Rick's Journal

Hope didn't return all at once. It came like dawn—quiet, patient, unhurried—slipping beneath the edges of everything until one morning I realized the cellar wasn't coming with me anymore. I left it in California. And somehow, I'm not afraid it will follow me across an ocean.

The plane touched down with a soft jolt, and the cabin filled with the shuffle of passengers waking and gathering their belongings. Marianne stirred beside Rick, stretching with a quiet sigh before her shoulder brushed his.

"We're here," she whispered, her voice still warm with sleep.

Rick smiled. "I know."

Even as he said it, the word meant more than geography. They were not just in London. They were at the beginning of something new.

Marianne must have sensed the shift in him because her eyes softened in that perceptive way that always made him feel seen rather than studied.

Passengers stood and reached for overhead bins. Months ago, Rick would have been on his feet instantly, scanning exits, measuring distances, preparing to move. Instead, he stayed where he was. Marianne's hand rested in his, and his body did not brace to run. He watched her tuck a loose curl behind her ear and felt no urgency to look away.

He was present. He was calm. He was married.

She caught him staring. "What are you smiling for?"

"You," he said honestly. "Everything."

Her blush crept in slow and warm. She nudged his knee. "You're impossible."

Heathrow greeted them in a blur of accents and winter-dim light, the air humming with motion and life. Rick kept their passports and bags close and Marianne laced her fingers through his as they followed the signs into the customs hall.

A man with a thick Manchester accent barked something about queuing properly. Rick startled only because he could not decipher a word of it.

Marianne laughed. "Welcome to England, Mr. Wentworth."

"Do they come with subtitles?"

"I'll translate," she promised, squeezing his arm.

The cab line was long, but neither of them minded. Marianne rested her head on his shoulder, and Rick let his cheek settle against her hair. When they finally slid into the back of a black cab, London's cold breath followed them before the door shut.

"Where to, lovebirds?" the driver asked.

Rick opened his mouth. Nothing came out.

"SoHo, please," Marianne supplied, grinning.

Outside the window, London unfurled—red buses, stone facades, the fading remnants of Christmas lights. Rick watched her more than the skyline. Wonder lit her face with every passing block.

"You okay?" she asked gently.

"Yes," he said, and the answer surprised him with its steadiness.

For the first time in his remembered life, that answer felt true without qualification.

The last time Rick had traveled far from home, fear had ridden every mile with him. Now, the memory barely stirred. He thanked God for that.

"I thought I'd be nervous," he admitted.

"And are you?"

He turned toward her. "No."

Her smile was tender and fierce all at once. "That's healing, Rick. That's God rewriting the page."

Emotion tightened in his throat. He had not known a moment could feel this quietly good.

The hotel in SoHo was elegant but warm—a brick exterior, soft lighting, a lobby that smelled faintly of cedar and cinnamon. Inside their suite, Marianne made a slow circle, taking in the tall windows, the four-poster bed, the velvet loveseat, and the oversized shower.

"Oh, Rick. It's perfect."

He did not look at the room. He looked at her and agreed happily. Those bright-eyed and radiant eyes were all he needed to see to know this was indeed perfection.

"When you look like that," he murmured, "it makes every penny of Darcy's worth it."

She arched an eyebrow. "Are you saying I'm expensive?"

"Yes," he said. "Utterly."

She laughed and stepped closer, cupping his face as she traced his smile with her fingertips. Satisfied with what she'd seen, her arms slid around his waist, and Rick lowered his forehead to hers inhaling her signature scent. Who would have thought something as simple as peppermint ChapStick could feel so intimate?

"You doing okay?" she asked softly.

Rick closed his eyes. For years, this kind of closeness had terrified him. He braced for panic and for memory to drag him under but none of that came. What came instead was a warmth and desire that made him gasp with delight as he opened his eyes.

"I'm good," he said quietly. "Better than good."

She brushed her thumb along his jaw. "We don't have to rush anything. You know that, right?"

"I know." He met her eyes. "But I'm not afraid, Marianne. Not now."

Relief, love, a fierce tenderness radiated from her open expression that made him want to raise his fist to the sky and shout for joy. She kissed his cheek, light as a vow.

"We have two whole weeks," she whispered. "Let's savor it."

They unpacked side by side with Marianne tucking away toiletries in the marble bathroom and Rick hanging their coats in the cavernous cupboard. Ellie's wedding card, two stick figures beaming beneath a sun, went on the fireplace mantel like a blessing.

Later, curled together on top of the duvet, Marianne rested her head on Rick's chest and traced slow circles along his arm.

"Rick?" she whispered.

"Yeah?"

"I'm really glad we're here."

He tightened his arm around her. "Me too. I've waited my whole life for this."

She angled up on her elbow. "London?"

"No." He kissed her hair. "Peace. You."

She did not answer. She did not need to. She simply curled closer, fitting against him as if they were learning each other anew.

And when sleep finally came, it did not come from collapse or exhaustion or the desperate hope of outrunning fear. It came from contentment and safety, from the way Rick's body finally believed in a future that belonged to them—one he intended to keep choosing, one day at a time.

CHAPTER THIRTY

Lucy had cried herself into an uneasy sleep hours earlier.

Her soft and uneven breathing drifted down the hallway, catching at the edges as though grief still hovered just beneath the surface of rest. Eddie had stayed in the old rocking chair beside the bed long after her shoulders stopped shaking, long after the nurse's discharge instructions blurred into meaningless sound. He stayed until Fanny touched his arm and whispered that she would sit with Lucy for a while, urging him to shower, to change his clothes, and to try and at least eat something.

Now he stood alone in the dim kitchen, both hands braced on the counter, staring at the mug of untouched tea he had poured out of habit.

The baby was gone.

He did not say it aloud. The words felt too final, too solid, as though naming the loss might lock it into place forever.

"Our son," he whispered. "My boy."

Grief did not roar in the Ferrars household. It settled heavy and dense, much as he imagined wet concrete would make it impossible to breathe deeply. Somewhere down the hall, a floorboard creaked. Fanny murmured something low and soothing, and the sound steadied him, in a way he had not been expecting, knowing that he was neither alone in the house nor alone in his marriage.

Eddie dropped into one of the kitchen chairs and leaned forward. His Bible lay open on the table, pages rumpled from where he had turned them earlier, searching for something firm enough to hold. The words swam instead.

He was not angry at God nor was he trying to run away. He just did not know how to even talk to God about this whole situation. Strangely enough, there weren't many examples in the Bible of grief following a miscarriage, he decided.

The memory of the hospital room pressed in on him as he remembered the sound of Lucy's trembling voice, her hands in his, the way she had leaned into him as if instinctively remembering something they had both almost forgotten.

I'm not leaving, he had told her. *Not tonight. Not ever.*

He meant it. Beneath the grief, something steadier had taken root. It was not peace but rather something more in line with resolve.

While he had been waiting under the harsh fluorescent lights for news of Lucy's condition, Eddie had come to understand something with painful clarity: drifting was no longer an option. Neither was silence disguised as gentleness going to be acceptable as he tried to fix their marriage. Lucy had not needed him to be careful these last few weeks. She had needed him to be present, fully and courageously, without escape routes.

That meant there could be no unfinished doors left open.

He pulled his phone from his pocket, staring at the dark screen as though unlocking it might open Pandora's box of consequences that he could no longer delay.

The phone buzzed against the counter.

Darcy.

He let it ring out. A moment later, a message appeared.

You don't have to talk. Just letting you know I'm here.

Eddie swallowed and typed back.

Later. I'll explain. Thank you.

Then he opened Elinor's thread.

Her last message still sat there—days old, written before the wedding, before the hospital, before everything had shattered and reassembled into something truer.

Are we okay? Please tell me we're okay.

His fingers trembled, but he typed anyway.

Elinor, it's Eddie.
I need to talk with you. In person.
Mrs. Jennings' Bakery. Thirty minutes.
If you can't, I understand. But this can't continue.

He sent it before he could soften it into ambiguity.

The reply came almost immediately.

Eddie stood and moved down the hallway. He paused at the bedroom door.

Lucy lay on her side, one hand curled near her face. Her lashes were still damp. The crease between her brows—the one that deepened when she was hurting—made something inside him ache.

Fanny looked up from the armchair, her Bible open on her lap.

"She asked for you once," she said gently. "But she's resting now."

"Will you stay while I'm gone?" he asked, his voice rough. "I won't be long."

"I'm not leaving her," Fanny said. Then, softly, "Are you all right, Eddie?"

"No," he said honestly. "But I'm choosing what's right."

Fanny nodded, her expression knowing. "I'll be here."

He brushed his fingers through Lucy's hair, careful not to wake her. "I'll be back," he whispered. "I promise."

She did not stir—but the urgency followed him all the way out the door.

The bakery was warm and quiet, the scent of yeast and sugar hanging in the air. Mrs. Jennings waved when she spotted him through the window.

Elinor sat at a table near the glass, hands wrapped around a paper cup of tea. She had already ordered one for him.

Her eyes were swollen. Her composure—once so carefully maintained—was cracked.

For a moment, the familiarity nearly undid him.

He sat.

"Thank you for coming," he said.

"Of course," she whispered. "I heard about the baby. I've been praying all night. I'm so sorry, Eddie."

"Thank you," he said. "We're taking it one breath at a time."

She hesitated. "I thought… maybe you needed someone who remembered you from before. Before things got so complicated."

He lifted a hand gently. "Elinor."

She stopped.

"This matters," he said quietly. "So I need to be clear—even if it hurts."

Her hands tightened around the cup.

"What we had in college was real," Eddie said. "You mattered to me. You helped shape who I became."

She exhaled shakily.

"But that season ended," he continued. "And I failed both you and my wife by letting old habits masquerade as kindness."

He met her eyes.

"Lucy is my wife," he said. "And she was the mother of my son."

Tears slipped down Elinor's cheeks.

"I love my wife," Eddie said, his voice steady. "And I am choosing her—not out of guilt, not out of obligation, but because she is who I belong to."

Her shoulders sagged.

"So this is goodbye," she said.

"Yes," he said. "To anything unresolved. Not to goodwill—but to hope that doesn't belong to us anymore."

She nodded slowly. "She must be extraordinary."

"She is," he said simply.

They did not touch. They did not linger.

The boundary stood.

When Eddie returned home, the house was dark and still.

Lucy woke as he sat beside her.

"Where did you go?" she asked, her fingers curling into his sleeve.

"I went to close a door," he said. "So I could stay where I belong."

Her eyes searched his.

"I choose you," he said quietly. "Only you."

Her breath caught. "Can you hold me?"

He gathered her into his arms without hesitation.

Later, under the porch light, Darcy held him as Eddie finally broke.

"I bought a onesie," Eddie sobbed. "He never wore it."

Darcy did not let go.

And for the first time, Eddie understood something he had spent years preaching but never fully lived.

Love was not proven by strength.

Sometimes it was proven by staying—broken, honest, and held.

Chapter Thirty-One

There was a time I didn't believe my body could belong to anything but survival. But tonight—in London, with Marianne's hand steady on my heart—I learned what it means to live without waiting for the dark. Peace can be loud or it can be a whisper. Tonight it was a whisper that felt stronger than chains.

By the time they made it back to the hotel, London had traded its pale afternoon for a soft blue-gray evening. Streetlights glowed like lanterns along the wet pavement. Taillights streaked red across the road, and from somewhere near the lobby doors, a busker's guitar floated faintly through the air.

Marianne slipped her hand into his as they crossed the lobby. Her thumb brushed the notch of his knuckles.

"Your face looks different," she said, teasing but curious.

"Different how?"

"You look… lighter."

He huffed a laugh. "I had three different cakes at tea. I think you meant to say *fatter*."

She nudged him with her shoulder. "It's not the sugar."

The elevator chimed, and they stepped inside, grateful there were no other guests crowding the matchstick-sized box the British called a lift.

"Halfway through the honeymoon," Marianne said lightly as they began their slow ascent to the sixth floor. "Any regrets about choosing London?"

"Not even one," he said, meaning far more than the city.

"Even with all the stairs?"

"Even with all the stairs," he agreed. "I don't regret anything about this trip, Marianne."

He meant it. For years, he had lived with an undercurrent of regret, tight beneath his ribs—the belief that there had been something he should have done to escape Louisa. Now he was standing in an elevator in London with his wife and could not find a single thing to worry about. It felt like a small miracle.

They reached their floor and walked the hallway in an easy silence. Her hand never left his.

He entered first, scanning the room, taking in the two armchairs, the low tea table, the bed turned down, and the city beyond the tall windows. There was no threat. Just them.

Behind him, Marianne kicked off her shoes with a groan. "My feet are filing for divorce."

"Denied," he laughed as he swung her into his arms. "You're stuck with them until death do us part. And me, too."

Her smile warmed the whole room when he tossed her onto the bedspread. "Best life sentence."

He set his wallet on the desk and checked the inside of his jacket until he found the folded hotel letterhead he had tucked there earlier.

Uncertainty rose as he peeked at the poem he had scrawled before they went out into the city. The last poem he had written for Marianne, on their first date, came from a man still afraid of his own reflection. This one came from a husband who was no longer afraid, as long as she stood beside him.

"I'm going to wash my face and change," she said lightly. "Unless you had something you wanted to share?"

"Why would you think I had something to share?" Rick stuttered, trying to hide the paper.

She laughed and playfully grabbed for it behind his back. Landing in a heap on the double bed, they tried to catch their breath, laughing as Marianne smoothed out the poem she had captured.

"Shall I read it, or will you?" she asked.

"I'll read it," he said. "That is, if you want me to. You might think it's silly."

She took his hand and handed back the paper. "There isn't a version of my life where I don't want to hear your words—even if they're silly."

He steadied the page, kissed her gently on the lips, and began.

London, with You
by Rick Wentworth

I used to think healing was quiet,
earned in empty rooms,
in long nights,
in the hush after fear,
in the way a man teaches himself to breathe
without an audience.

I thought it was solitary—
just me and God in the dark,
counting cracks in the ceiling
until the panic passed.

But then you laughed,
and the world tilted toward light.

London did too—
old stone and new glass
learning from you,
sipping tea like it's a small sacrament,
eyes bright over porcelain.

I realized healing sounds a lot like your voice
saying my name in places I never dreamed I'd stand,
feels like your hand finding mine without searching,
looks like a future with open windows,
curtains breathing in and out
as if we finally have air to spare.

*I once believed I had to bury the past
to be whole—
erase the cellar, the chains, the years.*

*But you—
you never asked me to be unbroken.
You only asked me to be here.
To stay.*

*To let you trace the scars without flinching,
to let your love live in the same body
that once knew only survival.*

*And now,
in a city older than my grief,
new as our vows,
I watch you across a table of crumbs and cold tea
and know:*

*Love isn't the absence of scars.
It's the presence of you
reaching for my hand—
in Croft Beach cafés with sticky menus,
in hospital waiting rooms,
in crowded churches and quiet kitchens,
on wet London sidewalks,
and in hotel rooms where I am finally
more husband than haunted thing.*

*If the past is a country I can't fully leave,
then let the future be this:
your laughter beside me,
your head on my shoulder,*

my fingers steady as they write our story,
one ordinary miracle at a time.

Not rescue.
Not escape.
Simply this—
London, with you,
and the quiet knowing
that I am already home.

When he finished, the room seemed to hold its breath. He lifted his eyes to her, suddenly unsure of his footing. Marianne blinked slowly, lashes wet, and looked at him with absolute love and joy.

"I don't have a word for what that is," she whispered.

"Too long?" he teased, because humor was still his last line of defense.

She laughed softly. "It's perfect."

"You're not proof of failure, Marianne," he said. "You're proof of grace."

Her lip trembled.

"I think the thing I liked best," she said, "was when you wrote that you're more husband than haunted thing."

"It's true," he said simply. "I wouldn't have believed it before we arrived in London. But tonight? It's true."

She brushed her fingers along his jaw. "Are you scared tonight?"

"A little," he admitted after a moment. "But not like I was last night. I'm not afraid of Louisa's shadow. I'm afraid of not loving you well enough. I'm sorry I couldn't," he said quietly. "I'm sorry I failed you last night."

"Not pleasing me? Failing me?" She gasped. "Rick, last night you pleased me beyond my wildest dreams. I was so happy I was tempted to cancel our plans and stay in bed all day. My only regret is that you didn't get as much pleasure as I did."

"I don't deserve you, sweetheart," he sighed. "You're my present and my future. And my body—I want to be with you so much it hurts."

Her cheeks warmed. "Are you blushing? Oh, Rick." Marianne sighed as she feathered kisses over his face. "You never have to be embarrassed with me."

They settled back against the pillows, shoulders brushing.

"Just because I'm all giddy and ready doesn't mean we have to rush," Marianne said. "We can sleep, read, talk. We have forever."

"I know." He paused. "But I'd like to try again tonight. If something feels wrong, I'll tell you. And you can too."

She pressed her lips to his shoulder. "Come here, husband."

He kissed her—slow, steady, anchored in the present. A flicker of shadow passed, but it did not cling. He breathed through it, let it dissolve, and returned to her warmth.

"You okay?" he asked once.

She smiled. "More than okay. You?"

"Still here," he said. "Still with you."

Every choice to remain present felt like a link snapping loose inside him. Joy—real joy—was beginning to live in his bones.

When they finally settled in the soft dark, her head resting beneath his chin, her hand over his ribs, he felt remade—exhausted, grateful, and unafraid.

"Hey," she murmured. "Was it okay for you?"

He let out a breath that sounded like wonder. "More than okay."

"How much more?"

He tipped her chin gently so she could see the truth in his eyes.

"It felt like proof," he said softly. "Proof that God didn't pull me out of the cellar just so I could survive. He brought me out so I could have this. You. Us."

Her tears slipped warm onto his skin.

"I love you," she whispered.

"I love you too," he murmured. "More than all the sand in California and all the bricks in London—and every terrible metaphor I could write."

She laughed against him, tired and happy.

"Poet."

He kissed her hair.

"Wife."

Outside, the city kept moving.

Inside, Rick Wentworth held the woman he loved, peace settling around them like a blessing he had once believed he would never feel. For the first time in his life, when he thought of his own body, the word that rose was not fear.

It was gratitude. And wonder. And a love so full it felt newly discovered.

Chapter Thirty-Two

Eddie had been halfway down the lawn when the mower sputtered and died.

He released the handle and stood there, hands braced on his hips, staring at the uneven stripes he had cut into the grass. The sudden quiet rang in his ears, sharp after the steady churn of the engine. He had not planned to mow that afternoon. He had come home from a short run—the kind he once relied on when movement was supposed to clear his head—and found the yard overgrown, the edges ragged and demanding attention. It had felt like something he could fix. Something with boundaries, with visible progress, with an ending.

His earlier run had not helped, and mowing was not doing any good either.

Eddie's grief neither lifted nor loosened. It simply settled heavier whenever he took a breath.

At a loss, he bent to check the mower, fiddling with the choke out of habit, then straightened again. From the corner of his eye, he noticed a car slowing at the curb. His shoulders tensed automatically, bracing for conversation, for concern, for well-meaning questions he did not yet know how to answer.

The car parked anyway.

Mrs. Alvarez climbed out, balancing a foil-covered casserole dish in one hand and a brown paper bag in the other. She wore sensible flats and a cardigan, her dark hair pulled back with one of her favorite bright plastic clips.

"Pastor," she called out cheerfully. "I hope I'm not interrupting."

"No, of course not," Eddie said, wiping his hands on his shorts and tugging his shirt straight. "It's good to see you."

She smiled, her expression soft without being pitying. "You do not have to pretend with me. I have five children, and one of them is an angel I hope to meet again one day."

"Yes," he said quietly. "I know." He hesitated. "You understand what we're going through."

"Sí." She nodded once and lifted the dish slightly. "I will leave this on your porch."

She walked past him and set the food down carefully, tucking the paper bag beside it so it would not tip. Eddie hovered nearby, unsure whether to help or simply stay out of the way.

"I did not know if you had dietary instructions yet," she said, straightening. "So it is plain chicken and rice, with broth on the side. Easy to reheat."

"Thank you," Eddie said. The words felt thin, but they were sincere. "You didn't have to—"

"I know," she said. "That is why we did."

He blinked. "We?"

Mrs. Alvarez glanced toward the street, where another car was slowing. "Caroline Darcy started a meal train online. You are not alone in this."

"A meal train," he repeated mechanically, as if the words belonged to a different language.

"Yes," she said. "Not just for this week, either. It looks like the schedule goes through until next month."

Eddie swallowed. "That's... incredibly generous."

Mrs. Alvarez touched his arm, gentle and sure. "Sometimes care does not wait for permission when the need is obvious."

He nodded, because nodding was easier than risking words that might crack him open in the middle of his front yard. As she turned back toward her car, he followed numbly.

Before getting in, she looked up at him, her eyes wet. "You are allowed to be a father who lost his child," she said quietly.

Eddie stared down at the concrete, at the scuffed toes of his running shoes. The mower sat abandoned behind him, a job half-finished and forgotten.

"Thank you," he said again, and this time the words carried weight.

After both she and his secretary, Mrs. Morland, had driven away, Eddie stood on the porch longer than necessary before carrying the dishes inside one at a time. The kitchen light felt too bright when he turned it on, so he dimmed it and set the chicken and rice casserole on the counter. The foil crinkled loudly in the quiet room. The smell of broth felt both ordinary and deeply out of place in a house suspended between before and after.

He opened the refrigerator and rearranged things mindlessly, sliding a jar of jam aside and nudging the milk back an inch, to make room for Mrs. Morland's cheesecake.

As he was closing the refrigerator door, he chanced to notice the flowers. A great variety of bouquets crowded the far end of the kitchen table, some in vases, others in baskets or small pots. He had not realized how many people had come by in the last few days.

His gaze flickered to a small stack of mail sitting on the table. Most of them were bills and advertisements, but what caught his attention was a card with the church's address on the envelope.

Inside, the message was simple.

Lighting a candle for you tonight.
We are holding you in our prayers.
—The Prayer Team

His throat tightened. Someone had thought of them standing in the dark.

Eddie set the card down and rested both hands on the counter, breathing slowly until the room steadied.

Turning off the kitchen light, Eddie walked down the hallway and found Lucy lying where he had left her, curled on her side, one hand tucked beneath her tear-streaked cheek. Her breathing was shallow but steady. The crease between her brows had eased, ever so slightly.

He stood in the doorway longer than he needed to, memorizing the rise and fall of her chest.

"I'll be back soon," he whispered, more to himself than to her.

She did not stir.

Eddie stepped inside and pulled a notepad from the dresser drawer.

Food's in the kitchen.
I'm going out for a bit. I'll be back.
I love you.

After placing the note where she would see it when she woke, he pulled out his phone and typed a quick message to his three o'clock appointment.

I'm stepping out for a bit but I'll give you a call later. Sorry for cancelling last minute.

Without stopping to consider what he was doing, he slipped his keys from the hall hook and closed the front door gently behind him.

Outside, the late afternoon light had softened. The air smelled of cut grass and something faintly sweet. Standing on the porch for a moment, keys warm in his palm, Eddie allowed himself to feel the weight he was carrying without trying to outrun it.

Then he walked next door to the church.

The side door creaked softly as he pushed it open. The sanctuary was cool and dim, the stained glass glowing rather than blazing. Eddie walked down the aisle and stopped at the small table near the front where candles waited in glass holders.

It had taken months to convince the elders to create this space. He had been so certain he was advocating for others at the time. The possibility that he might one day need it himself had never occurred to him when he'd argued for the prayer corner.

His hands shook so badly as he picked up a candle that it took two tries to light it. The flame flickered, then steadied.

"You are here," he whispered into the vastness of the room. "You never left."

His voice broke, and Eddie bowed his head as he stumbled backwards onto a pew. Tears came quietly at first, then harder. His breath stuttered as grief finally moved instead of being contained.

"I don't know how to do this," he moaned. "My mind keeps reaching for reasons You never promised were true."

The candle burned on.

A soft click sounded behind him.

Eddie did not turn immediately. He wiped his face and drew in a breath before looking back.

George Knightley sat down in the front pew, his cane resting against his good leg, his gaze lifted toward the cross.

They sat together without speaking.

After a long while, George said quietly, "Do you know Psalm Twenty-Three?"

Eddie closed his eyes in thought.

"Even though I walk through the valley of the shadow of death, I will fear no evil," he quoted softly. "For you are with me; your rod and your staff, they comfort me."

"I guess as a pastor you're required to know that passage," George said with a half-smile. "But for me it was the only prayer I had left after Emma and our baby died. I don't say that it explained everything away, but rather it reminded me I was not walking alone."

Eddie stared to the front of the sanctuary.

"I keep wondering if this happened because I sinned," Eddie admitted. "What if I did something that made God turn away and punish us?"

George shook his head. "You don't believe that."

Eddie let out a breath he did not realize he had been holding. George was right. In his heart and soul, he did not believe that. However, when he was at his lowest point, it sure made sense. As he tried to make sense of his state of mind, Eddie's ache remained, but it settled into something he could carry.

They sat together in the quiet, two men who had buried too much, held by the small, steady light that did not desert them as Eddie understood that he did not have to hold the grief alone.

Chapter Thirty-Three

I am healing.

Rick had not expected the countryside to feel so different from the city, but as the taxi carried them deeper into the heart of Somerset, the change drew him in more mile by mile. London had been vibrant and exhilarating, its noise and movement acting as a kind of electric balm he had not known he needed. This landscape offered something else entirely. Narrow lanes wound through open fields and hedgerows that stood like old sentinels, and the winter sun cast a pale gold across the hills. It was spacious without feeling exposed.

Rick rested his arm along the back of the seat and let himself breathe.

Marianne slept with her head on his shoulder, her hair tickling his jaw every time the car curved gently with the road. After only two weeks of marriage, the familiarity of the moment surprised him. It felt as if they had been in an intimate relationship for years instead of weeks. Wherever they were going, the world felt manageable with her beside him.

She stirred when the Georgian manor came into view, its honey-colored stone glowing softly against the fading afternoon light.

"Are we here?" she asked, her voice thick with sleep.

"Just about," he murmured, pressing a kiss to her cheek.

She smiled and straightened as the car pulled to a stop, the cold air crisp as they stepped out. Before they reached the front steps, the door swung open.

"Finally," Caroline exclaimed, pulling both of them into a hug that felt like home. She stepped back and studied them with exaggerated seriousness. "You two look disgustingly happy. And extremely married."

Rick laughed. "London was incredible. We can't thank you both enough."

Darcy appeared behind his wife, smiling broadly. "Rick, my friend, you look ten years younger."

"I feel it," Rick admitted. He hesitated, then added, "I haven't had a single nightmare or panic attack since our second night of the honeymoon in London."

Darcy's expression softened as he slipped an arm around Caroline's shoulders and ushered them inside. The warmth of the house wrapped around Rick immediately, and he wondered how long it had been since he had felt this unguarded.

They moved through rooms lit by soft lamps and quiet conversation, the house welcoming without ceremony. When they reached the bedroom, Marianne paused, hands resting at her sides as she took in the space.

"That bed looks dangerously comfortable," she said with a grin.

Rick stepped behind her and pulled her back against him. "We should probably test that theory with a nap."

She turned to kiss him, but before their lips met, a sharp knock echoed from downstairs. They both froze, Marianne's fingers tightening briefly in his sleeve.

"The house is empty," Marianne said.

Rick nodded. "We better check to see who it is."

They reached the entryway just as the door opened to reveal Eddie and Lucy.

Eddie stood with a single suitcase at his side, his shoulders drawn inward as though he were bracing against a weight he could not set down. Lucy stood beside him wrapped in a shawl, her face pale and drawn, her eyes shadowed with an exhaustion that Rick recognized immediately.

Marianne crossed the space without hesitation and gathered Lucy into her arms. Lucy sagged into the embrace, her body yielding as though it had been waiting for permission to stop holding itself upright.

Rick moved to Eddie and pulled him into a firm hug. Eddie's breath caught audibly as he allowed himself to be held, his fingers gripping the back of Rick's jacket.

"I'm glad you made it," Rick murmured as he thumped Eddie's back.

Eddie swallowed hard. "We needed this more than I can say."

"I know," Rick replied. "And we're not letting you carry it alone."

Darcy returned with Caroline just as Ned and Fanny came in from town, and the house filled quickly with familiar voices.

"Let me take your bags," Darcy said, already reaching for Eddie's suitcase, while Caroline and Fanny made a big to-do over Lucy.

Rick lingered a moment, watching Lucy settle into the cushions of a loveseat. He thought of the video call Marianne had taken that morning, of Elinor's quiet decision not to move to Croft Beach permanently after all. It felt like several chapters were closing at once.

As Fanny passed around cups of tea, she paused near the hearth instead of returning to her seat.

"Before we all scatter," she said gently, "I want to say something about the week ahead."

The room quieted.

"This week isn't a rigid program where anyone is expected to arrive broken and leave fixed," Fanny continued. "Some days will be heavier. Others will feel lighter. We've planned it that way on purpose." She smiled faintly. "We'll have time for group discussion and other times for each couple to get out and away from the group. And we even have a few really fun planned outings that I think you're all going to enjoy."

A few shoulders eased.

"If at any point something feels like too much," she added, "you're allowed to step away. This week isn't about pushing through. It's about staying present and getting closer to God, to your spouse, and to each other."

Ned nodded from his chair. "I hope this week gives all of us room to breathe," he added simply.

Marianne's hand slid into Rick's, and he squeezed it lightly. Across the room, Eddie reached for Lucy's hand. Darcy leaned back with his arm around Caroline, the lines of his body easy and unguarded.

Rick took in the scene slowly. No one was fixing anything. No one was rushing grief or forcing joy. They were simply four couples who were present together, sharing the moment.

"May I propose a toast to this week—and the Bertrams' generosity?" Rick said impulsively, lifting his teacup with a smile. "I think I speak for all of us when I say I believe God is going to use this time for the good of every one of us, right where we are."

Chapter Thirty-Four

Eddie woke before dawn, momentarily disoriented by the soft blue walls and the faint birdsong drifting through the old shutters. It took him a minute to remember they were in Bath. He was far from home, far from the hospital, far from the night everything broke open. Then he rolled over and saw Lucy.

She lay curled on her side, wrapped in the brown shawl she had used on the plane. Her breathing was soft but uneven, shaped by the kind of grief that sleeps without ever truly resting. One hand rested over her stomach. Even in sleep, she looked breakable in a way that carved him open.

He whispered a quiet prayer. "Lord, please help me keep showing up."

By breakfast, the house hummed with the gentle noise of sleepy voices, clinking tea cups, and the rustle of newspapers as toast was buttered. Lucy perched on a barstool by the kitchen counter, small and folded inward, her shawl wrapped tightly around her shoulders. Eddie sat beside her, present in the quiet way he wished he had learned sooner.

After they had eaten, Ned called everyone to gather in the comfortable sitting room. Once everyone had settled in the room, Ned smiled around the group and began. "We'll start simple today so no need to start sweating. Each couple will be responsible for naming one thing that hurts. I know that this part can be uncomfortable. If it helps, remember that you're not here to solve anything today. We just want to speak the truth and let it sit."

Eddie felt Lucy tremble and drew her closer. When he looked up, he caught Ned's eye and saw an open invitation.

"Eddie," Ned asked gently, "would you begin?"

Eddie inhaled slowly and managed a strained smile. "Nothing like starting with the heavy hitters. I was hoping we'd begin with easier questions—like what our favorite colors are."

Ned chuckled. "I'll remember that one for later. We all know you and Lucy have carried a great deal of pain these past weeks. Could you name one wound you're holding?"

Eddie looked around the room before answering. "I'm here because I want to become a man who doesn't let words fail him when they matter most," he said. "I want Lucy to feel supported and to know she is not abandoned because of my passivity or silence. If I had to put it into one word, it would probably be *sensibility*. I grow uncomfortable when emotions rise up, especially when I can't control the outcome."

Lucy opened her eyes. They glistened with unshed tears, but what startled him was the way she reached for him. Her hand extended, steady and open.

When Ned invited her to speak, Lucy took a slow breath but did not let go of Eddie's hand. "As you all know, I'm grieving," she whispered. "Deeply. And I'm so tired. Naming a wound feels harder than I expected."

Her voice wavered. "I think my wound is the fear of being abandoned. I don't know where it began. I had a happy childhood with no obvious trauma. And yet I've always been afraid of being left behind. Elinor's visit in Croft Beach tore that fear wide open."

Eddie felt the words land in his chest like both a blade and a calling and saw Marianne, sitting across from him, flinch just as sharply as he did.

"But I came here," Lucy added more firmly, "because I believe God has something sacred still waiting for Eddie and me. Our baby left us early… too early. I feared Eddie would leave me but I never imagined our baby would leave me. It's all just…"

With a faint smile, Lucy sat back and squeezed Eddie's hand as Ned moved on. Darcy and Caroline went next, followed by Rick and Marianne and lastly Ned and Fanny. Darcy named pride. Rick spoke of control. Ned shared that he was struggling with being shortsighted. Eddie listened to everyone, recognizing the familiar shapes of old battles spoken aloud.

Fanny released a quiet sigh and glanced around the room. "I don't know about the rest of you," she said, her voice warm, "but I'm relieved to remember that perfection was already taken care of. By Jesus."

A ripple of amusement moved through the room as everyone sat back a little easier. Kissing his wife with affection, Ned grinned. "What would I do without this angel?" With a wink to Fanny, he picked up loose paper he'd brought with him and started passing the pages out. "In one sentence, we want everyone to name the wound you just shared with the group and your specific goal for this retreat. Only your spouse will read it so you should hopefully feel comfortable putting it down on paper."

Eddie picked up the pen and wrote:

My wound is sensibility, and I came here because I never want to put you in a position where you feel abandoned or second to anything in my life. My prayer is that I learn not to run away from feelings.

Lucy wrote beside him, then handed him her paper with trembling fingers.

Lucy's words struck him with quiet force as he read it once and then once more. He folded the paper carefully and slipped it into his wallet next to the photo he kept of Lucy.

Ned said nothing for a long moment. Then, quietly, he asked, "Does anyone want to share anything today before Fanny introduces our fun activity for the day?"

Eddie had not intended to stand. However, Eddie found himself suddenly in the center of the room with every face turned toward him. For a moment, he could not speak.

"I bought a hat," he said finally.

Darcy inhaled sharply. Lucy gasped.

"It was a tiny baby hat," Eddie continued. "I bought it the day I finally let myself believe I was going to be a father. I gave it to Lucy when I came home, and for the first time, it felt like our lives were realigning." His voice broke. "Then we lost him. And I've been afraid of so many things. But mainly I think I'm afraid that maybe, somehow, I am to blame."

He crossed the room and lowered himself at Lucy's knees, resting his head in her lap.

"I'm scared," he whispered. "I can't lose you. I've made more mistakes than I can count, but I want to be the husband you need. I want to love you so completely that you never have to fear abandonment again."

Her arms came around him without hesitation. In her embrace, the grief finally moved instead of stagnating. Though they were thousands of miles from Croft Beach, Eddie felt like he had found home.

That night, in their room, Lucy lay beneath the covers while Eddie stood by the dresser, holding the suitcase with careful, reverent hands. He removed the baby hat and placed it gently in her lap, like an offering.

After a long silence, she spoke. "I want to keep trying to fix us."

His breath shuddered.

"I'm not promising it will be easy," she continued. "Or that trust will come easily for either of us. But I want to fight for our marriage too."

He nodded and moved toward her, reverent, careful, until he was a breath away. Then he lowered his head and kissed her.

"I'm here," Eddie whispered. "And I'm ready to become the man you need."

She hesitated, then lifted the covers beside her. Eddie slid into bed, overwhelmed by the comfort of her touch as she curled into his arms and reached to turn off the lamp.

Darkness settled gently over the room, holding Eddie and Lucy in the quiet, steady presence of God, where fear no longer lived.

CHAPTER THIRTY-FIVE

There are mornings when I wake up and feel the weight of the cellar like a shadow at my back. And then there are mornings like today—soft light, steady breath beside me—when I realize resurrection doesn't always come with trumpets. Sometimes it comes with peace that feels almost ordinary. Almost holy.

Rick had just settled onto the low stone wall near the garden when the screen lit up.

Before he could speak, a chorus of voices burst through.

"Dad!"
"Daddy!"
"Hi!"
"Is that really him?"
"Hey Brother Rick!"

George's voice cut in, laughing. "All right, all right—one at a time. He's not going anywhere."

The image steadied enough for Rick to make them all out. Sam leaned closest, his face filling the screen with serious concentration.

Walter hovered just behind him, bouncing on the balls of his feet. Lily waved both hands enthusiastically, her hair half-falling out of its tie. Ellie was perched sideways on George's knee, clutching Quackers by the wing and grinning so hard Rick felt it in his chest.

"There you are," Rick said, smiling so wide it almost hurt. "I was wondering when you'd all find me."

"You're outside," Maggie observed immediately. "Why are you outside? Is it cold? Have you seen the King yet? Are you with my sister?"

Rick chuckled. "Slow down, guys. Yes, I'm outside. It's cool, but not cold. And no, we haven't seen the King since you asked us that a couple days ago."

George groaned theatrically. "Has it only been a couple days? How much longer do I have to hang out with these kiddos?"

"Dad," Sam said, cutting through the laughter, his brow furrowed. "Are you okay?"

Rick met his son's eyes and answered honestly. "Yeah. I really am."

Sam nodded once, satisfied.

"What is there to do in Bath?" Walter asked. "Mom Marianne said there was a lot of walking trails."

"There are," Rick said. "Marianne and I went on a long one this morning in fact."

Lily leaned closer to the screen. "Do you miss us?"

Rick didn't hesitate. "Every minute."

Ellie held Quackers up to the screen. "Quackers misses you!"

Rick laughed softly. "I can tell."

George shifted Ellie higher on his knee. "We're holding things together here," he said. "Maggie's put all of Marianne's clothes and shoes in the closet, Sam's in charge of making sure homework actually happens, Walter's been alphabetizing Marianne's seasonings in the pantry—"

"I was helping," Walter protested.

"And Lily's supervising everyone," George finished. "Ellie of course is everyone's favorite cheerleader."

Ellie beamed.

"What did you do today?" Maggie asked. "Like, what was your favorite part?"

Rick glanced down at the small parcel resting beside him on the stone. "Actually… Pastor Fanny gave me something that made me think of all of you."

He held the photograph up to the camera.

For a moment, the screen went quiet.

"That's us," Lily breathed.

Sam leaned in closer. "We look… different."

Rick swallowed. "I guess we do. I didn't realize she had taken it."

George nodded slowly. "Fanny has a good eye."

Ellie tapped the screen. "You're holding me."

"Yep. And all of you are holding me."

Maggie smiled, her voice gentler now. "That's a great picture of all of you."

George cleared his throat lightly. "All right, team. Let's let your dad enjoy the rest of his afternoon."

"We love you," Lily said quickly.

"See you soon," Walter added.

Sam gave a small nod. "Proud of you, Dad."

Ellie blew an exaggerated kiss and waved Quackers again.

When the screen went dark, Rick sat very still, the photograph warm in his hands.

Healing, he realized, didn't always announce itself. Sometimes it was a moment frozen in time with the knowledge that the people who held you there were still waiting when you came back.

Rick was still turning the photograph over in his hands when Marianne joined him on the low wall.

"I couldn't resist watching you from the upstairs bedroom window," she admitted. "I'm guessing they haven't burned the house down yet?"

Chuckling, Rick shook his head. "Everyone is doing well," he said. "Sam called you 'Mom Marianne.'"

Her smile softened, something warm and surprised flickering across her face. "Did he?"

"He said it like it was the most natural thing in the world," Rick replied. "No hesitation."

Marianne sat beside him, their shoulders brushing. "No matter how much I detest that woman and what she did to you all, I would never want to replace her in the kids' lives," she said quietly.

"You're not," Rick said at once. "They are choosing you. Just like how you are choosing us."

She glanced at the photograph in his hands. "Is that the one Fanny gave you?"

He nodded and turned it so she could see. "I didn't know she'd taken it. I didn't even realize that was happening—until I saw it."

Marianne studied the image for a long moment. "You look… loved," she said.

"I felt loved," Rick answered. "I don't know how one man can be so fortunate."

She reached for his free hand, lacing her fingers through his. "And what about the fear?" she asked quietly. "The last eleven years don't just disappear."

Rick breathed out slowly. "I think that's what today is teaching me. When I try to control everything, I panic. When I focus on what I can't undo, it builds until I can't breathe."

"I never thanked you," Rick said after a moment.

Marianne turned toward him. "For what?"

"For London," he said. "When I froze. You didn't push. You didn't make it about what we couldn't do. You stayed."

Her grip tightened slightly.

"You showed me I didn't have to force my way through fear to be loved," he said. "That mattered more than you know."

"I married all of you," she said softly. "That night included."

Emotion pressed hard against his chest. "I know. I just wanted you to hear it."

They sat quietly for a few breaths.

"What do you need from me," Rick asked, "when fear shows up for you?"

Marianne considered the question. "I think I need to say something out loud before disappointment starts writing a story I don't want to believe."

He listened.

"I don't expect poetry all the time," she continued. "Life is loud. The kids are real. I don't want to measure your love by how often it looks romantic."

He smiled faintly. "But you'll miss it."

She smiled back. "I love that part of you. I just don't want to doubt us when love looks quiet."

Rick squeezed her hand. "Then let me be intentional—even when I'm not poetic. Once a month, I'll plan something. No distractions. Just us."

"Once a month," she said thoughtfully. "I can work with that."

"And the rest of the time," he added, "you'll have a man who chooses you and shows up—even when it's ordinary."

"That's the part I'm trusting now," she said.

They stayed there a while longer, the photograph resting between them, the afternoon light shifting slowly around their feet. Peace was no longer something to brace for, but something they were learning to live inside.

Chapter Thirty-Six

Eddie first noticed the change when Lucy laughed. It was quiet and unguarded, the kind of sound that surprised them both. The laughter faded quickly, but it left something behind. There was now a lightness that had not been there before.

They were standing near the window in the sitting room, sunlight slipping through the glass in pale ribbons, when Caroline made an offhand comment about English weather and Lucy's lips curved before she could stop herself.

It was not the brittle brightness of forced cheer, or even the fragile politeness she had worn since the miscarriage, but something warmer and steadier that suggested possibility.

Eddie watched her carefully, afraid that if he looked too hard, it might disappear. She caught him watching and smiled, as if to say she felt it too.

Ned clapped his hands together gently. "No heavy work today. You've all earned a break."

Eddie could feel Lucy's shoulders ease at the words.

"This city," Ned continued, gesturing toward the window, "has been a place of restoration for centuries. Water, beauty, and stillness have done their work here for a very long time. I thought we might let them do what they have always done."

Fanny grinned. "Which is Ned's long-winded way of saying that we are all going to the spa."

There was a beat of surprised silence before laughter rippled through the room.

"All of us?" Darcy asked skeptically.

"All of you," Fanny confirmed. "Couples' massages followed by dinner dates we have arranged at some of Bath's most romantic spots. Everything has been pre-booked and paid for. All you have to do is pull a slip of paper from the basket to see where you will be dining tonight."

Ned smiled. "That is probably the hardest thing you have to do so have at it, friends."

Lucy let out another small laugh, this one freer than the first, and Eddie couldn't resist grinning with her.

Darcy and Caroline went first, drawing a slip that said they were going to be dining tonight at Fanny's favorite hotel on the iconic Royal Crescent. When it was Eddie and Lucy's turn, he let Lucy reach into the basket. She read the card and gasped.

"The Pump Room," she said, then squealed outright and kissed his cheek.

Eddie laughed, wishing he could take credit for the choice. The joy on her face was more than enough.

He had been nervous about having a stranger's hands all over his body, but Eddie could have easily fallen asleep during their fifty-minute session. Lying on the table across from Lucy, he felt the tension ease from his shoulders as skilled hands worked carefully and respectfully, as though even his body needed reassurance that it was safe to rest. His breathing slowed without effort, each exhale longer than the last.

He glanced at Lucy. Her eyes were closed, her face peaceful in a way he had not seen in months. She looked like someone who was no longer bracing herself for the next wave of grief.

When their hands brushed afterward, she laced her fingers through his without hesitation.

"I forgot what it felt like to just be," she murmured.

He squeezed her hand. "Me too."

When they emerged from the treatment rooms, wrapped in plush white robes, the staff guided them up a narrow staircase toward the rooftop. The open-air pool stretched out before them, steam rising gently into the cool afternoon air, the city of Bath unfolding below like a living painting.

Darcy was the first to spot them. He was already waist-deep in the water beside Caroline, his hair damp and his expression suspiciously relaxed.

"Well," he said, lifting an arm along the edge of the pool, "I take back every unkind thing I have ever said about spa culture."

Rick laughed as he stepped closer, Marianne tucked comfortably against his side. "You were the one who said it sounded unnecessary."

"It was unnecessary," Darcy replied easily. "Until it was not."

Eddie lowered himself into the water beside Lucy, the warmth wrapping around them both. She leaned back against his chest without hesitation, her head resting lightly against his shoulder, and he felt the quiet miracle of that trust settle in.

Beside him, Rick closed his eyes with a low exhale. "I am just saying that if this is what happens after one afternoon, I am prepared to make this a weekly spiritual discipline."

Fanny raised an eyebrow. "Of course you are."

Ned chuckled, easing himself down beside her. "I seem to recall someone who was afraid of being touched, and now look at you."

Rick opened one eye. "This feels otherworldly."

Marianne laughed, the sound musical to Eddie's ears. "You are not getting a standing weekly massage appointment, Mr. Wentworth, on a teacher's salary."

Darcy glanced at Caroline, one corner of his mouth lifting as he dunked her playfully in the water. "Speak for yourselves. I feel called, and I think Caroline and I should be making this a weekly date night."

Ignoring the other couples' amusement, Darcy grinned at Caroline as if she hung the moon and leaned in to kiss her cheek. Her braids drenched from the dunking she'd received, Caroline growled at Darcy and jumped on his back dunking him in return.

"You go, Caroline Darcy!" Marianne giggled as she high fived the other woman.

Caroline rolled her eyes affectionately as she tried to squeeze excess water from her braids. "Just wait until you are knee-deep in a case, Mr. Darcy, and cannot even make it home for dinner."

Lucy giggled softly, the sound freer than it had been in days. "I think the rule should be that none of you are allowed to mock us

womenfolk about manicures, pedicures, or spa treatments ever
again.”

Eddie smiled down at her. “I am just grateful you never felt the
need to change a single thing about yourself—especially your
eyelashes, Sweetheart. They have always been perfect to me.”

Lucy gasped, blushed fiercely, and turned away as Eddie grinned
and caught supportive nods and amused grins from his friends.

That evening, Eddie took her to the Pump Room Restaurant. As
they stepped inside, candlelight glowed against cream-colored walls,
and the hum of quiet conversation wrapped the space in warmth.
Soft music drifted from somewhere unseen, barely rising above the
clink of silverware and low laughter.

Lucy wore a simple dress, her hair loosely pinned at the nape of her
neck. She had chosen it carefully and Eddie didn’t think she had
ever looked more beautiful. Eddie pulled out her chair, waiting
until she was settled before sitting across from her. For a moment,
they simply looked at each other, both smiling a little, as if
surprised by how significant this was.

“Well,” Lucy said lightly, glancing around, “I think Fanny and Ned
knew exactly what they were doing.”

He chuckled. “I suspect the basket was rigged.”

“I wouldn’t even mind if it was,” she said. “This feels like a gift.”

They talked easily over dinner about everything from the retreat
sessions to the spa date earlier in the day, and about how strange it
felt to let someone else decide the evening for them.

“I didn’t realize how tired I was of choosing,” Lucy admitted.

"Makes complete sense to me. We've been going non-stop. At least for me, I've been trying so hard to make sure everything worked out that I forgot how to simply receive moments like this. It was a relief today to just be told what to do and receive things like this beautiful dinner out."

"Do you remember," he continued cautiously, "how surprised we were when Caroline started the meal train list?"

"I don't think surprised is even close to how I felt." Lucy grinned in remembrance. "Finding that pot of soup and Mrs. Morland's cheesecake in the kitchen that first night was like Christmas morning."

Lucy's smile softened as she shook her head. "I remember standing there thinking I must be mistaken. I told myself that surely it couldn't be all for us. And then I froze realizing the ways people had shown up already, without being asked or needing explanations."

She traced the rim of her glass with her fingertip. "I didn't have words for it then, but I think that was the first moment I believed we might survive what we were walking through. Not because it hurt less, but because we weren't going through it alone."

Eddie swallowed past the sudden tightness in his throat. "You never told me that."

"I didn't know how," she admitted. "I was still trying to be strong. I didn't want to be vulnerable." She met his eyes. "I don't want to hide anymore."

He reached across the table and covered her hand with his. "Neither do I."

Their server appeared with fresh glasses of wine, setting them down with a quiet smile before retreating. Eddie lifted his glass without quite thinking it through, then paused.

Lucy noticed. "What?"

He smiled, a little sheepish. "I was going to say something, but now I'm worried it'll sound like a sermon."

She laughed softly. "You are literally a pastor. I think we can allow it."

He exhaled, then raised his glass up.

"To Fanny and Ned," he said. "For knowing when to step in and when to step back."

Lucy lifted her glass too.

"And to our friends," Eddie continued, his voice steady but warm. "For meals we didn't earn, prayers we didn't ask for, and hope they carried for us when we couldn't manage it ourselves."

Lucy's eyes shone. "To you, my husband and lover," she said quietly. "And to learning how to stop hiding from each other."

Their glasses touched with a soft clink.

Eddie took a sip, then smiled at her over the rim. "You know," he said, "if the basket *was* rigged, I'm not mad about it."

"Me neither," Lucy said. "I think this might be my favorite assignment yet."

"Let's promise ourselves when we go home to Croft Beach that we don't lose what we have found here," she continued softly.

He nodded. "It's a promise."

After dinner, they walked hand in hand together toward the Bath Abbey, the stone glowing gold in the fading light. Lucy slowed as they approached, her steps instinctively angling toward the open doors.

"This wasn't on the list," she said quietly.

"No," Eddie agreed. "But it feels right."

The evensong service was already beginning when they slipped inside, music filling the vaulted space with something ancient and steady. They found a place near the back and sat side by side, allowing the choral music to wash over them.

The cleric spoke of mercy, renewal, and a love that endured as a commitment to remain.

When the service ended, Lucy turned to Eddie, her eyes bright. "Thank you for today," she said. "For trusting the process. For trusting me."

They walked back to the house, hands entwined, the city dimming behind them. Lucy hummed softly, and Eddie realized that hope did not announce itself with certainty or promises. Sometimes hope arrived as a lightness in the chest, sometimes as a shared silence that did not ache, and sometimes as the simple knowledge that grief had not won.

CHAPTER THIRTY-SEVEN

Rick had never intended for anyone else to hear these words.

They had been written in the quiet hours when the house still slept and on long walks where memory pressed close. He had folded the page away each time, telling himself it was enough that God had heard it.

But now the room was full, and the words would not stay hidden. As he watched Darcy and Caroline playfully bicker about treacle sponge versus sticky toffee pudding, and saw Fanny scribbling madly on her yellow pad while Ned leaned close to murmur something that made her laugh, a conviction settled over him. Not a suggestion. A calling.

Lucy had drawn Marianne aside, asking her something with that shy, earnest smile, and Rick felt it then—clear and insistent.

Now.

He turned on his heel and hurried upstairs. From his Bible, he pulled the poem he had been shaping all week, scanned the lines once, then tucked the folded pages into his shirt pocket before heading back down.

Eddie sat nearest the hearth, hands wrapped around a mug of tea. His shoulders still carried grief, but he sat upright now, the mug steady in his hands. Seeing the way Eddie had been changed for the good this week only strengthened Rick's resolve. Tomorrow, they would all return to London and then on to Croft Beach for Easter. There would not be another moment like this.

Marianne crossed the room and slipped her arm around his waist. "Everything okay?" she whispered.

"Perfect," he murmured.

Her eyes flicked to the folded page peeking from his pocket, her eyebrow lifting in quiet curiosity.

He never found out what she was going to ask.

Ned stepped forward and clapped his hands lightly. "All right, everyone. It's our final night. I know we've gone through a lot, but I thought it might be meaningful if we—"

This was it.

Rick stepped forward, interrupting with a blush. "Sorry, Ned—but I wrote something this week, and I was hoping I could read it."

The room stilled.

Ned glanced at Fanny, then smiled and swept his hand outward. "The floor is yours."

Rick unfolded the pages.

And began to read.

The Cost of Sensibility
by Rick Wentworth

I once was half agony,
dragged to a cellar where light obeyed her hand—
flicked on or off at whim,
a cruel reminder that even the sun
was not mine to choose.

Drugged to make me usable,
though my soul refused consent.
The world may say a man cannot be taken,
but I was.

A virgin bound, reduced, despised—
and yet, by mercy, preserved.

From violence came a fragile cry,
Lily's breath against my chest.
Not born of love,
but still beloved—
God's mercy in the midnight hour.

Three times more I held new life,
babies pressed into my arms,
only to feel them torn away,
again, again, again.

Each loss a wound deeper than chains.
Each silence another burial of hope.

The cost was agony.
The years, the chains, the nights that mocked me.
The lie that said I was less than a man,
less than a father,
less than free.

But God was not absent.
He preserved my children.
He preserved me.

Now those same arms that once bore iron
are circled by children's laughter.
Their hugs around my neck
redeem what the collar once defiled.

What Louisa meant for evil,
the Lord has redeemed for good.

The cost was high—
a decade lost,
a man undone.

But the gift is greater still:
their smiles,
their trust,
their future unchained.

And grace gave me more:

Marianne—
the one a small-minded town
called too different,
too far outside their polished lines.

But she is my joy,
my healing song,
the bride of my heart,
the wife of my soul.

I would not stand here whole today
without the brother who never ceased to pray,
who never gave up when hope seemed gone,
who carried me through the trembling dawn.

Darcy—my anchor, my fiercest friend,
you held my hand when nights would not end.
Through panic's grip, through haunted cries,
you stayed beside me, steady, wise.

And Eddie—
I have seen your struggle too,
the cost of sensibility in betrayal's flame.
Desire without covenant devours,
but mercy, still, calls us home.

Your story reminds me:
grace is not just for the captive,
but for the one who has strayed.

So I stand here,
a husband,
a father,
a brother,
a man remade.

Half agony, yes—
for scars do not vanish.

But half hope, too—
for love remains,
for Christ sustains.

And this—
this is my testimony:

That chains can break.
That scars can heal.
That love can rise from ruin.

This is my testimony:
That Christ redeems what sin destroys.
That mercy outlasts the night.
That grace is stronger than shame.

This is my testimony:
That I was half agony,
but He made me half hope—

And in His hands,
wholly free.
Forever free.
Always free.

In Christ,
eternally free.

When Rick lifted his eyes, the room seemed to hold a single, fragile breath.

Marianne wept openly, her hands clutched at her heart. Caroline swiped mascara streaks with the heel of her palm. Darcy stared into the fire like he had been carrying the weight of Rick's pain in his own chest for years.

And Eddie stood. He simply rose, crossed the room with tears gathering at the corners of his eyes, and wrapped Rick in a tight, trembling bear hug.

Rick didn't hesitate. He held him back.

Eddie's voice shook. "Thank you… for telling the truth. For not sparing me. For seeing me."

Rick swallowed hard. "Same, brother. Same."

Lucy stepped forward and clasped her husband's hand as she wiped tears with her sleeve. Her gaze on Rick was tender, loving, and even grateful.

Ned cleared his throat, visibly steadying himself. "Thank you for trusting us with that."

Fanny sniffed. "Next time warn us to wear waterproof mascara."

Soft laughter rippled through the room as Marianne tucked herself into Rick's side and rested her head against his shoulder. "You never fail to amaze me," she whispered.

Ned raised his mug. "To Rick, and to the courage it takes to speak when silence would be easier."

The fire crackled softly. The old house seemed to exhale. Warmth wrapped around them like a blessing.

Tomorrow, they would head back to Croft Beach. Tomorrow, real life would meet them at the door. But tonight, in the golden hush of their last evening in Bath, they rested in the truth that God had met them here fully, tenderly, and completely.

Rick looked out the window one last time, the lamps glowing against stone that had stood for centuries.

The cost had been great, but grace—always—was greater still.

CHAPTER THIRTY-EIGHT

The sanctuary smelled like lilies and polished wood. Easter morning in Croft Beach Community Church always was one of Rick's favorite times of the year but this year everything felt different, better even.

Sun poured through the stained-glass windows in long bands of color, warming the pews instead of merely illuminating them. Rick stood beside Marianne in a pew near the center aisle, her hand resting easily in his. When she glanced up at him, her smile was unguarded.

"You okay?" she whispered.

Rick nodded once. "Yeah. I really am."

Beside them, the kids fidgeted in familiar ways. Lily adjusted the crooked headband in her hair. Rick could make out Walter whispering urgently something about chocolate eggs. Sam bounced on his heels, barely able to contain his excitement for lunch. Ellie stood between Rick and Caroline Darcy, Quackers tucked under one arm, the duck sporting a pastel bow tie Caroline had sewn the night before.

Rick leaned down. "You look very dignified today, Little Love."

Ellie grinned. "Aunt Caroline said I'm a duck princess."

"I believe it," Rick said solemnly.

The organ swelled, and the congregation rose as one to sing.

Christ the Lord is risen today…

Rick closed his eyes as the hymn filled the sanctuary. His shoulders stayed relaxed. His breath stayed steady. When the final chord rang out, he realized that nothing inside him had tightened.

Had so much changed in a little over a year?

A few spaces over, Darcy stood beside Caroline, his thumb brushing over her knuckles as they sang. Rick caught Darcy's eye and lifted his chin in a small nod. Darcy returned it, something proud and grateful passing between them.

When the congregation sat, Rick turned slightly and caught sight of Eddie and Lucy across the aisle. Lucy stood close to Eddie, her light blue shawl brushing his arm. Her hand rested in his and Eddie looked ten years younger.

Ned stepped to the pulpit. Rick straightened instinctively, the way he always did when a sermon was about to begin. Easter sermons were predictable in the best way with themes of joy, safety, and hope.

"Christ is risen," Ned said, his voice warm and steady.

"He is risen indeed," the congregation replied.

Ned smiled, then closed his Bible.

Rick blinked as he watched Ned pick his Bible up and hand it to Fanny.

"I planned to preach this morning," Ned said. "Easter has always been one of my favorite times to preach. However…" A ripple of quiet amusement moved through the room. "It so happens that something else has become just as clear to me."

Ned turned slightly, his gaze settling across the aisle.

"Eddie Ferrars, can you join me please?"

Rick felt Marianne's fingers tighten around his hand.

Eddie looked up, startled, but at Lucy's nudging slowly started to make his way to the podium where Ned held out his hand.

"You took a sabbatical this year for a few months," Ned continued. "No one here should ever imagine that because your pastor took some time off that he's not worthy of his calling to lead here at Croft Beach Community Church."

The sanctuary was very still.

"Eddie Ferrars is one of the most wonderful men of God I have ever had the privilege of calling my friend and of sharing a pulpit with."

Rick swallowed hard as he saw where this was leading.

When Eddie reached the front, Ned didn't speak again. He simply pulled him into a firm embrace—one man to another, pastor to pastor—then Ned stepped aside to go and sit with Fanny in the front pew next to Lucy.

Rick felt something shift in his chest as Eddie stepped forward, and declared, "Christ is risen." His voice was warm and sure.

"He is risen indeed," the congregation replied with a hint of amusement as Eddie thumbed through his Bible and found the passage he would read from.

After the sermon, as the final hymn faded, Eddie closed his Bible and looked out over the congregation.

"Before we go," he said, "I want to say this."

"Resurrection isn't always loud," Eddie continued. "Sometimes it's simply a man choosing to stand where God has placed him again despite fears and scars."

"Some of you might know that the Darcys, Wentworths, Bertrams and Lucy and myself went away for a week. It was truly amazing. And while we were there one of the things that touched me the most was a poem that Rick Wentworth wrote and read for us. And Rick, I was wondering if you'd consider reading a part of it for everyone?"

Rick lifted his head, his jaw dropping in shock.

He nodded and stepped forward, his shoes sounding too loud in the sudden quiet. He paused at the front, resting his hands lightly on the pulpit.

"Hey, everyone," he began awkwardly into the microphone. "I obviously wasn't expecting anything like this so didn't bring the poem with me."

A ripple of laughter passed through the sanctuary lightening the tension in Rick's shoulders.

"But thankfully I did memorize a portion of the poem which I am guessing Pastor Eddie was referring to so with your indulgence, folks, this is a small section from my poem, *The Cost of Sensibility*:

So I stand here,
a husband,
a father,
a brother,
a man remade.

Half agony, yes—
for scars do not vanish.

But half hope, too—
for love remains,
for Christ sustains.

And this—
this is my testimony:

That chains can break.
That scars can heal.
That love can rise from ruin.

This is my testimony:
That Christ redeems what sin destroys.
That mercy outlasts the night.
That grace is stronger than shame.

This is my testimony:
That I was half agony,
but He made me half hope—

And in His hands,
wholly free.
Forever free.
Always free.

In Christ,
eternally free."

Much like the other night in Bath when Rick had read his full poem, the room was completely silent. Then the congregation was on their feet giving a thunderous applause as Rick staggered back in shock. Eddie threw his arm around his shoulders and whispered, "I can never thank you enough, Rick."

As the congregation rose and the music swelled again, Eddie pulled Lucy into his arms and kissed her gently as Rick stepped back into the crowd to return to Marianne and the children.

"You did well," she said quietly.

He nodded. "I never imagined I'd be reading anything I wrote up front."

She considered that, then nodded once. "It may not be your ideal but you're definitely gifted. Guess it goes to show you'll be terrific tomorrow when you start teaching at Jane Austen Academy."

Outside, bells rang as people spilled into the courtyard. Children darted around eager for the egg hunt to commence. Rick scooped Ellie up, spinning her around once before setting her down. Lily offered Marianne a daisy, which she tucked behind her ear with a giggle of pleasure.

Eddie stood beside Lucy near the steps, watching the chaos unfold.

Rick approached them, smiling. "You participating in the egg hunt?"

Lucy smiled faintly. "We'll watch this year."

Rick nodded. "That counts."

"Seriously?" Darcy groaned dramatically behind Rick. "Here I signed up for the actual egg hunt and got a basket too and all I needed to do was come watch?"

Laughing at her husband, Caroline shook her head in amusement as Ellie came running up to her for a hug. Tickling Ellie, Caroline grinned up at Rick and said, "Don't forget. Faculty meeting's early tomorrow. You don't want to tire out before your first day of teaching."

Rick smiled. "I won't. I feel like a kid I'm so excited."

"He's had his backpack ready for weeks now!" Sam groaned which was answered by a chorus of laughter by the adults.

They stood together as sunlight warmed the stone beneath their
feet, bells ringing overhead, and children ran around in the grass.

EPILOGUE

Fifteen Years Later

Rick walked the shoreline alone as the sun dipped toward the horizon, the sky rinsed in gold and rose and softening blue.

Croft Beach had not changed much. The rhythm of the waves was the same. The scent of salt still clung to the air. But everything else—everything that mattered—had moved forward in ways he could never have imagined.

Ahead, near the place where the sand sloped gently toward the water, he saw her.

His beautiful daughter sat with her skirt spread around her like fallen petals, careless of the wet sand. Her hair was half-loosened, the careful pins abandoned. The veil lay beside her, forgotten.

Rick stopped walking.

For a moment, he only watched. Lily, his eldest child, was no longer the girl who once clutched his shirt in fear, no longer the small voice that had anchored him to the world. She was twenty-five now. She was a bride who would not be walking down the aisle tonight.

He approached slowly, giving her time to sense him.

"I thought you might come find me," Lily said without looking up.

Rick lowered himself beside her, the hem of his trousers darkening as the tide crept in. "I got your S-O-S."

She stared out at the water. "He called it off."

Rick didn't speak.

"He says he's only half whole now," she continued, her voice thin
with tightly held emotion. "The accident. The chair. The scars."
She swallowed. "He says I deserve someone unbroken."

Rick closed his eyes briefly.

"He thinks love is measured by what hasn't been lost," Lily said.
"By symmetry. By ease."

She finally turned toward him, mascara streaked, eyes brave and
aching. "Is he right?"

"No," Rick said gently. "But he's afraid. And fear lies
convincingly."

Lily's hands tightened in the ruins of her dress. "I don't know how
to help him see that."

Rick studied her face—the woman she had become, the courage
she carried without yet knowing where it had been forged. The
memories pressed close, old and heavy and sacred.

It's time, he thought.
Not tonight. Not all at once.
But soon.

"There are some stories," Rick said carefully, "that change how we
understand suffering. How we learn to heal. And what it really
costs to love someone."

She searched his eyes. "What stories?"

He looked back out at the water. "Not yet."

The sun slipped fully below the horizon, the first stars pricking the sky.

Rick reached for his daughter's hand, just as he had when she was small. She took his without hesitation.

"Do you remember the first sunset we ever watched together at the beach?" he asked.

"First sunset?" Lily said, incredulous. "Here in Croft Beach?"

He smiled faintly and squeezed her hand. "No. We were on our way here—years ago. Your Uncle Darcy pulled off at a public beach up north, and I carried you down to the water. You watched the sun disappear into the ocean from my arms."

"Up north?" Lily frowned. "I don't remember living anywhere else. I must have been little."

"You were nine," Rick said quietly.

She looked up at him, startled.

"When we get home," he added gently, "there's something I want to give you."

The waves moved steadily in and out, faithful as breath.

Some love stories began in joy.
Others began in truth.

And his love for his daughter had begun the moment she was placed in his arms.

A Letter to My Readers

Dear friend,

If you're reading this, it means we've reached the end of a journey we stepped into together—one that began with a broken man in a cellar and ends with a whole man standing in the light.

When I first wrote Half Agony, Half Hope, I didn't know exactly where Rick's path would lead or how many lives he would touch. I only knew this:

His story mattered.
And so did yours.

Long before this trilogy had a title, God placed Rick's story on my heart with a weight I couldn't ignore. I felt called—deeply and unmistakably—to write a narrative that honored survivors, upheld the dignity of men who suffer in silence, and testified to a God who restores what evil attempts to destroy.

I knew my mission:

- *to encourage,*

- *to give hope,*

- *to speak life into hurting hearts,*

- *and to build stories where grace is louder than shame.*

That mission has been the foundation of my encouragement platform—The Joyous Living, The Joyous Author, every post, every devotional, every whispered reminder that hope really does return with the tide.

Through this trilogy, we've walked with Rick through trauma, fatherhood, healing, and the terrifying beauty of choosing love again. We watched Darcy stand beside him like a lighthouse. We witnessed Eddie and Lucy wrestle with failure, forgiveness, and the slow miracle of redemption.

And through it all, one truth kept rising to the surface:

No story is beyond the reach of God's grace.

If Rick's journey has spoken to you in any way, my prayer is that it whispered something personal:

• Your scars do not disqualify you.
• Your past does not define you.
• Your worth is not up for debate.
• Your healing is not impossible.
• Your story is not over.

Thank you—truly—for letting these characters step into your life. For reading their prayers, their panic, their humor, their victories. For cheering when Rick finally learned to breathe again. For holding space for Eddie and Lucy's heartbreak. For loving Marianne, Caroline, and the whole Croft Beach community that feels like home.

This may be the final chapter of Rick's trilogy, but it is not the final chapter of this world. More stories are coming—full of grace, joy, second chances, restored marriages, growing families, and the stubborn hope God keeps writing in the margins of our lives.

But this book—*this ending*—belongs to Rick.

To the man who thought he'd never be whole.
To the father who feared he wasn't enough.
To the survivor who believed he was beyond repair.
To the husband who learned that love doesn't demand
perfection—only presence.

Thank you for every message, every prayer, every review, and every
time you shared these stories with someone who needed
encouragement. Thank you for walking beside me in this mission
God planted so clearly on my heart.

As Rick would say:

*"Half agony. Half hope. And somehow—by grace—
wholly free."*

Here's to joy.
Here's to hope.
Here's to the next beginning waiting just beyond this page.

With so much love and gratitude,
Joy
The Joyous Author

Author's Note on Trauma & Hope

If you've walked with Rick from <u>Half Agony, Half Hope</u> all the way to this moment, then you already know this:

His story isn't just fiction.

It is a reflection—a mirror for anyone who has endured pain they didn't choose, wounds they didn't deserve, or losses that felt too heavy for one heart to hold.

When I first wrote Rick's story in *Half Agony, Half Hope*, I had no idea I would someday write a devotional called *Wholly Free*. I didn't know his journey would become a vessel through which God could speak into places where shame hides. I didn't know how many readers would quietly whisper, *"Me too,"* when they recognized their own pain in his.

I only knew this:

Trauma demands honesty.
Healing demands hope.
And God is present in both.

Rick's story has touched some of the hardest realities a person can face—abuse, fear, grief, betrayal, loneliness, and the long, quiet work of rebuilding trust. These themes are tender. Sacred. And many of you reading this have walked your own dark valleys.

If that is you, let me speak directly to your heart:

You are not alone.
You are not forgotten.
You are not beyond healing.

Trauma does not make you less worthy of love.
It does not make you less deserving of joy.
And it absolutely does not place you outside the reach of God's
mercy.

One of the most powerful truths I've learned—personally, and
through writing Rick—is this:

God never wastes suffering.
He transforms it.
He redeems it.
He walks through it with us.

The devotional *Wholly Free* was born out of that truth. It grew
from the realization that Rick's fictional journey was echoing
something deeply real and universal: the slow, grace-filled process
of becoming whole after life has shattered us.

And friend, hear this clearly:

Wholeness is possible.
Freedom is possible.
Restoration is possible.

This does not mean the journey is quick or simple.
It does not mean the scars disappear.
It does not mean faith erases what happened.

But it *does* mean that God steps into the story with you—right
where you are—and refuses to let pain be the final word.

If Rick's story has met you in a tender place, I hope it gently
reminds you of these truths:

• Healing isn't linear.
• Grief is not a failure of faith.
• Asking for help is courage, not weakness.
• Your story matters—deeply.
• God can redeem even what feels unredeemable.
• Restoration may be slow, but it is real.
• Hope is stubborn and steady.
• Freedom often comes in layers—and each layer is worth celebrating.

And above all:

You are worthy of love, safety, belonging, and joy.

If you need encouragement on your own journey, *Wholly Free* is there for you—not as an appendix to Rick's story, but as a companion for your own. It was written with the same heart behind these novels: to uplift, to point to Christ, and to remind you that grace speaks louder than shame.

Thank you for reading.
Thank you for trusting me with these sacred themes.
Thank you for allowing Rick's story to walk alongside your own.

May you go forward with hope—
not because everything is perfect,
but because God is faithful.

With love and gentle encouragement,
Joy
The Joyous Author

DID YOU LIKE THIS BOOK?

If *The Weight of Prejudice* inspired you, encouraged you, or simply kept you turning pages late into the night—would you consider leaving a review?

Your words matter more than you know. Reviews help other readers discover new stories and give indie authors like me the chance to keep writing, sharing, and growing.

Whether it's one sentence or a thoughtful reflection, your voice makes a difference.

Leave a review on Amazon, Goodreads, or wherever you buy your books.

Thank you for reading. Thank you for feeling. Thank you for sharing this journey with Darcy, Caroline, Rick, and Marianne.

With gratitude,
Joy Michelle Austin

COMING MARCH 17, 2026

HALF AGONY, HALF HOPE: THE DEAR LILY EDITION

A NEW, GENTLE NOVEL TOLD THROUGH A FATHER AND DAUGHTER—TWENTY-FIVE YEARS APART

On February 28, 2025, Rick and his children were rescued.

Sixteen years later, his daughter Lily stands at the edge of her own story—grappling with questions from a childhood she barely remembers, scars she cannot yet explain, and a love being tested by fear.

Half Agony, Half Hope: The Dear Lily Edition is not simply a revised version of the original novel. It is a **new, reimagined story**, told through **two interwoven points of view**:

- **Rick's past**, written during the days of captivity and rescue—where survival, faith, and fatherhood were forged under unimaginable pressure
- **Lily's present**, sixteen years later—where love, identity, and truth collide as she begins to understand the cost of her father's courage

This edition preserves the heart of Rick's journey—courage, healing, redemption, and hope—while gently fading to black during the darkest moments. Trauma is handled with care, restraint, and reverence, allowing readers to experience the story without graphic detail.

Written for readers who longed to step into Rick's world but found the original too intense, **The Dear Lily Edition** offers a tender, layered narrative designed with protection in mind.

ESPECIALLY SUITED FOR:

- older teens (with parental discretion)
- trauma-sensitive readers
- tender-hearted readers
- readers on their own healing journey
- fans of fade-to-black fiction

WHY THIS EDITION EXISTS

Some stories are meant to be told in full.
Others are meant to be shared gently—and at the right time.

Over the past year, readers asked for a version they could safely return to, recommend, or share with loved ones who could not endure the intensity of the original. **The Dear Lily Edition** was created out of love for those readers—and in honor of the daughter whose love reshaped Rick's life.

This edition allows readers to witness the miracle of rescue **and** the long echo of healing—
walking side-by-side with Rick and Lily Wentworth.

FOR READERS WHO WANT:

• the heart of Rick's transformation
• Lily's voice and her coming-of-age faith journey
• the enduring bond between father and daughter
• the beginnings of love, trust, and hope
• a gentle, fade-to-black reading experience

This story is for you.

———

A FATHER'S LOVE.

A DAUGHTER'S BECOMING.

ONE RESCUE—TWO STORIES—SIXTEEN YEARS APART.

Return to Croft Beach and walk once more with Rick, Lily, Walter, Sam, and Ellie—
this time through Lily's eyes, guided by the quiet, steadfast love of a father who never stopped protecting her heart.

HALF AGONY, HALF HOPE: THE DEAR LILY EDITION
Releasing March 17, 2026

**Because some stories deserve to be told softly—
and some truths are best discovered with time.**